The Dunwich Horrors Die Tonight

Hangman's Jam
Volume II

by

Rob Errera

The Dunwich Horrors Die Tonight, Hangman's Jam, Volume II
© 2020 Rob Errera
roberrera.com

Bad Hound Press
A Division of Giant Dog Books
BadHoundPress.com

Editorial guidance by Dominic Wilde and Ken Kimmel

Cover design by Dominic Wilde

ISBN-13: 978-1-949043-14-3

CHAPTER ONE

Surrender

"Vinny. Wake up. Mom and Dad are dead."

"What?" Vinny rubbed his face, wiping away sleep. *What did Vance say?*

"Pegdick. On the couch downstairs. Cold and blue," Vance said. He sat on the end of Vinny's bed, near the window, blowing cigarette smoke through the screen. "They've been that way for at least an hour."

"Did you call someone? The police?" Vinny jumped out of bed so fast, the ensuing head rush threatened to take him back down. He put his hand against the wall.

"I waited to wake you."

"Jesus, Vance! Why?"

"There's no rush, Vin," His twin brother sounded calm, amused. "Go downstairs. See for yourself."

Vinny took the steps two at a time, socks slipping on the hardwood. Dad lay in the living room recliner; Mom on the couch. Dad looked asleep, except he wasn't breathing, his face blue, mouth drooping at an odd angle. Mom looked worse, eyes open, lips foamy. A slimy trail of fluid ran from her mouth, to the couch, to a puddle on the floor. A tiny Bunsen burner, tin foil, and empty plastic baggies cloudy with residue crowded the top of the coffee table.

"Fuck," Vinny said, running a hand through his hair. He should have seen this coming. Peggy and Richard Boyle had gone from Bohemian free spirits to full-blown junkies over the last six months. Vinny hoped it was a passing phase. He'd seen his parents get in deep and pull themselves out before. Hell, Pegdick were wasted for as long as he could remember. Mom and Dad's "special medicine" was a running gag between Vinny and Vance since they'd learned to talk. Now the joke was over.

"I woke up an hour ago and found them like this." Vance took a swig from a water bottle. "I made some pancakes. Do you want some?"

"No. You...you made pancakes?" Vinny asked. "Why didn't you call someone? Why didn't you wake me up?"

"I tried but you were really crashed," Vance explained. "I practiced oboe for a while. I finally got that run down, you know, the fast one in E? Then I got hungry, so I made pancakes."

Vinny looked from his brother to his dead parents. The puddle of Mom's vomit-drool was nearly dry, her skin as gray as an old wasp's nest.

"There was nothing I could do. Nothing you could, either. It's the final voyage of Pegdick," Vance said. Vinny hated his brother's lopsided leer. "They're gone, Vinny. I'm sorry for our loss. But music...food..."

"Did you take your medication today, Vance?"

Vance waved his hand and turned back to the kitchen.

"Pancakes?" he asked again.

"Have you taken your meds at all this week?" Vinny asked. "This month?"

"Fuck that shit, Vin," Vance said. "It messes up the music."

"Bro, you're fucking bi-polar! Or borderline personality. Or schizophrenic. Maybe all of the above. Nobody knows *what* the hell is wrong with you, Vance. But *something* is wrong. You need to take your medication." Vinny pointed toward the living room. "Our parents are lying dead in there, man, and you don't even feel anything!"

Vance put a cast-iron skillet on the stovetop and lit a flame beneath it. He pulled a bowl of batter from the fridge and worked it with a whisk. Vinny waited for his brother to meet his eyes, but Vance remained fixated on breakfast prep. Everybody deals with grief differently, or so Vinny heard. Was his brother in shock? Was this a side effect of his medication (or lack thereof)?

Vance had grown more unpredictable, more aggressive, since graduating high school last year. His mental decline mirrored their parents' downward spiral. Maybe Vance was right, maybe doctors were bullshit, an endless plunge into medication—drugs, drugs, and more drugs—all designed to make you someone you weren't, someone society demand you be. Standing between the kitchen and the living room, staring at the back of his dead parents' heads, Vinny wished he could turn the clock back to a time before his brother's diagnosis, back when a temper tantrum was merely a way for a boy to blow off steam. But angry boys become angry men and what happens then?

Richard Boyle's bald spot winked above the top of the recliner. Vinny's father fought a losing battle with hair loss for years, but when did Peggy get so gray? Vinny remembered her hair as jet black, cascading over the driver's seat in an ebony wave, an oil spill. He sat in the backseat of the car as a child, watching it sway and ripple, and, if he positioned the seatbelt just right, he could reach out and touch it, so magically soft and silky beneath his fingertips.

"Stop fiddling with my hair! I'm trying to drive!" Peggy chided from the front seat, but Vinny didn't stop, and his mother always allowed it, knowing the texture of her hair soothed and comforted Vinny like a baby's blanket. Mom always knew. Now her hair was as lifeless as the rest of her.

"Christ, Vance. We have to call someone." Vinny rubbed his face again, fingers coming away wet with tears. "We need to call… an ambulance…"

"We should call Mr. Phillips," Vance said, carefully pouring even circles of pancake batter onto the hot skillet.

"Who?"

"Howard Phillips."

"Your oboe teacher? The judge from the recital last year?"

"He's not my oboe teacher. He runs the studio where I take lessons. But yeah."

"Why would we call him?"

"He's Pegdick's drug dealer. Well, a teacher at the studio is a dealer, not Mr. Phillips himself. Mom takes me there once a week to cop."

"You're kidding?"

"No. What kind of shitty joke is that?"

"Christ, what the hell did Phillips sell them?" Vinny glanced at the empty baggies. "Coke? Meth?"

"Beats me," Vance said, flipping pancakes. "They used to snort it, but they started smoking it about a month ago. Didn't you notice?"

"I…no."

"What kind of son are you? You don't even notice when your dear old parents switch addictions," Vance said with a wink. "Face it, Vinny. This has been a long time coming. Mom and Dad were druggie losers."

"They loved us, Vance!"

"Did they? Maybe years ago, when we were kids. Our musical abilities made them look good, but, really, what did they have to do with it?"

"They paid for all those damn piano lessons!" Vinny said. "And we inherited our musical talent from them. Dad played guitar and Mom had a beautiful singing voice. They could have been successful musicians if they didn't have to raise us."

"Maybe, Vinny, but I think it's just as likely they would have ended up in a gutter someplace, as dead and disgusting as they are now. They're losers, Vin!"

"Shut up! They did their best! They were good parents! So what if they drank and did drugs. Can you blame them? All the shit we put them through. All the shit *you* put them through?"

Vance flipped a pancake.

"Do you think they're dead because of me, Vinny?" Vance asked. "Do you think I killed Mom and Dad? Or did they die because they were drug addicts? Because they were weak?"

"They were people, Vance. People who did their best." Vinny stifled a sob. He hated crying in front of Vance. Vance cried all the time, without shame, but the equation didn't work in reverse. Vance scooped the finished pancakes onto a plate and poured another round.

"They tried. I'll give you that," Vance said. "But they failed. Look at them!"

"Christ, Vance. They were human beings. They were our parents."

"They used to be. Now they're lying around, stinking up the furniture. Not much different from when they were alive, actually."

"Stop it, Vance," Vinny sniffled. "We need to call the police."

"Call Mr. Phillips first."

"That guy killed our parents, Vance!" Vinny's head throbbed. "Why the hell would we call *him*? We should give his name to the cops!"

"Call him first. As a courtesy."

"What fucking courtesy? What are you talking about?"

"Mr. Phillips can help us."

"How?"

"He warned me this might happen," Vance said, working the grill. "We saw Pegdick going downhill."

"Vance, look at me," Vinny said.

Vance scooped another batch of pancakes off the grill and deftly plated them. He pushed the plate toward Vinny and locked eyes with his brother.

"I've learned a lot at Mr. Phillips' studio," Vance said. "Sit down. Eat."

"Vinny, our parents are dead! We need to call the police!"

"Well, they're not going to get any livelier on an empty stomach!"

"Vance!"

"But…," Vance held up a finger dramatically as he placed a bottle of maple syrup next to the plate of pancakes. "Our parents *may* get livelier —as in, *alive again* — if you chill out a second and let me tell you about the work I'm doing with Mr. Phillips."

"What work? Drug dealing?"

"Sit down."

Vinny sat in the chair opposite his brother. The pancakes smelled warm and delicious, but it seemed disrespectful to eat with their parents lying dead a few feet away. They really did smell wonderful, though. The pancakes, not their parents.

"Howard Phillips is a facilitator. He makes things

happen."

"Like what?" Vinny asked. He pulled the pancakes closer. It'd be a shame to let them go cold.

"Howard Phillips knows people who know people who know…things," Vance said. "Ancient wisdom, Vin. The secrets of the universe."

"What are you talking about, Vance?" Vinny said. "You see, *this* is why you need to take your damn meds! This is word salad. Mom said the doctors called it that. It's nonsense babble. You're not making sense, Vance."

"You're not listening, Vinny," Vance replied. Vinny's heart raced. His brother appeared completely calm and lucid and it terrified him. "What if I told you Mr. Phillips can bring Mom and Dad back from the dead?"

"I'd say we need to call the police, Vance," Vinny said, sneaking a pancake from the bottom of the stack and nibbling the edge. "Delusions and hallucinations are common among mentally ill people who *don't take their fucking medicine*."

Vance gave Vinny a sad smile.

"Got me there, bro. I'm nuts," Vance said. He opened the syrup bottle and squeezed a puddle onto the plate. Vinny dipped in. "That's why we should call Mr. Phillips. Let him explain."

"Sorry, Vance, but we need to call the police first," Vinny said. He crammed the rest of the pancake into his mouth and pulled another from the stack. Vance knew his way around a flapjack. "Peggy and Rich were our parents. We need to be respectful and do the right thing. We should have called the cops already."

"Okay. Okay, we'll call the police, tell them we woke up and found them like this. That's true," Vance said. "But think it through, Vin. The cops find our parents overdosed in the living room, surrounded by drug paraphernalia. Is that what you want? Shouldn't we let Phillips come and clean this stuff up first?"

"No, we can't hide what happened," Vinny said. "Mr. Phillips should be arrested."

"Okay, so the police come. They bag up the evidence and take Mom and Dad away. The next time we see them, they're in caskets. We bury them in the ground and never see them again."

"That's the way it usually works when people die, Van," Vinny said. He couldn't look at his parents, but he nodded in the direction of the living room. "It's sad but true."

"What if it didn't have to be that way?" Vance said, his eyes as bright and crazy as a jack-o-lantern. "What if Mr. Phillips brings Mom and Dad back?"

"Who is Mr. Phillips, Van?" Vinny asked. "Jesus Christ?"

Vance considered this.

"No…he's a writer, I think," Vance said. "But he's a man of many talents. A resourceful man."

Vinny stared at his brother until Vance spoke again.

"I've *met* them, Vinny," Vance said, leaning close to his brother. "I've *met* reanimated people. They're quite pleasant."

Vinny shook his head.

"Sure you have, Vance. I was at a zombie picnic with Frankenstein last week." Vinny sighed. With Mom and Dad gone, he was Vance's keeper now. In a way, he supposed he always had been. "Take your medicine, bro, and let's not miss next week's therapy appointment, okay?"

Anger flared behind Vance's eyes but disappeared in an instant.

"Brad Pennysmith is a zombie," Vance said. "He plays bass for No Quarter out of Dallas. I met him twice. He's a nice guy. He died of an overdose two years ago and Mr. Phillips brought him back."

"Vance, I don't know who told you this story, or why you believe it, but it's bullshit," Vinny said. "Those douchebags at Phillips' studio are taking advantage of you, making fun of your disability."

"I don't have a disability!" Vance said. "I have amazing abilities. And I've met dead musicians who are still alive and walking around, thanks to Mr. Phillips."

"How does he do it?" Vinny asked. "Voodoo rituals?"

Vance shrugged, not sure if his brother was teasing him.

"With music," Vance said. "And magic…"

"And a steaming pile of unicorn shit," Vinny said. "Look, Van, I want to believe Mom and Dad can come back, but that doesn't happen. That's not the way life works."

"Can't we at least call Mr. Phillips?" Vance asked. "Don't Mom and Dad deserve that chance? Doesn't our family deserve it?"

Vinny scowled at his brother.

"A minute ago you called our parents assholes and now you're a family man?" Vinny said. "Make up your mind, you bi-polar numbskull."

Vance blushed.

"Okay, so we call the police," Vance said. "They take our parents away and disgrace our family. How long before they take away the house?"

"We're eighteen," Vinny sighed again. "Maybe we can keep the house."

"How will we pay for it?"

"We get jobs, brainiac."

"That's right, rocket scientist," Vance said. "Mr. Phillips can get us jobs. We can teach at his studio, or maybe he'll get us into a band."

"How do you know he'll give us jobs?" Vinny asked. "I barely know the guy beyond shaking his hand at the recital last year."

"He remembers you," Vance said, but didn't elaborate. "He can get us jobs in the music industry. He's a record producer and band manager. That's what he does!"

"I thought he ran a rehearsal studio," Vinny said. "Or is he a drug dealer? Or a talent show judge? Who the hell is this guy really, Vance?"

"Howard Phillips is different things to different people," Vance said, pulling a pack of cigarettes from his pocket. He tapped one out and tossed the pack on the countertop before lighting up. "He's a man who can help us, Vinny. We need help. Especially now. *I* need help, Vin."

"You're not supposed to smoke in the house," Vinny said.

"*Our* house now," Vance said, glancing toward the living room. "Let's try to keep it that way, Vinny. Let me call Howard Phillips."

Vinny extracted a cigarette from the pack and Vance lit it for him before flicking ash onto the dirty pancake plate. Vinny rubbed his temples and exhaled a cloud of smoke. It felt weird smoking in his parents' kitchen, rebellious and dirty.

"What kind of jobs does Mr. Phillips have?" Vinny asked.

"Won't know until I call him," Vance replied. "But he knows people."

"Yeah," Vinny said. "People who know people who know … things."

Vance and Vincent Boyle smoked their cigarettes down to the filters, drowning the smoldering butts in a tiny lake of maple syrup.

CHAPTER TWO

Ful Stop

"Boys, I'd like you to meet your new drummer...Brad Thomas," Howard Phillips said.

Chubby with thick-lensed glasses and a t-shirt that read Franz Rock Performing Arts Center, Brad Thomas stuck out his hand. Vinny grabbed Brad's hand and crushed his pudgy fingers. Judging from the pained expression on Brad's face, Vance did the same.

"Uh...hi," Brad said. "I'm looking forward to jamming with you guys. I hear you're good players."

"The Boyle brothers are two of the most talented musicians you'll ever meet. Both boys got full scholarships and graduated near the top of their class at Chancellor Academy," Howard said, standing between Vinny and Vance, laying a hand on each of their shoulders. Vinny stepped away from Howard's frozen, deadwood hand. He hated when Howard spoke like he was their father. The more time he spent with Howard Phillips, the more Vinny came to appreciate Richard Boyle's stoned, never-there parenting style.

"Cool. I went to Franz Rock PAC," Brad said. He launched into a lengthy dissertation on the talents and techniques of Buddy Rich, Ringo Starr, and Neil Peart until Howard cut him off.

"We're playing Hungarian dances today," Howard said, handing out sheet music. "Brahms. Enchanting melodies with a true, Old European folk feel. Good luck, boys. Don't mess up."

Vance played piano, Vinny, electric viola. Howard introduced him to the instrument a month ago and Vinny took to it immediately. With four strings and an endless array of tones, the viola was a breeze to play compared to the piano, yet Vinny found its deep, sonorous voice doubly expressive.

Brad Thomas took his place on the drum throne behind a sparse kit loaded with accessories—roto-toms, chimes, bells, dozens of cymbals...even a shiny gold gong. He clicked his sticks together and the music began.

They played all 21 dances, getting a feel for the pieces. The second time through, they cut loose. Vance improvised for twelve bars during Dance No. 6 and Brad gave the familiar No. 5 a metal kick drum drive. Vinny thought they sounded good, but Howard Phillips was unimpressed.

"Sloppy! Sloppy! Slop-slop!" Howard said, hands flapping around his head like angry hornets. Brad set his sticks down on his floor tom and folded his hands in his lap. Vinny cradled his viola on a stand, while Vance stood from behind the piano and stretched until his back cracked. From the way his brother scratched his shoulders and craned his neck, Vinny knew Vance needed a cigarette. He wanted one too. Hopefully Howard's ass-chewing would be brief.

"Your kick's late in every song, Brad!" Howard chided, his eyes filled with straight hate. Brad flushed deep red. "Work your chops. Woodshed! And Vance, I don't appreciate you deviating from the assigned sheet music.

There will be time enough for improvisation when we get to jazz. This is about precision. Play the notes on the pages as written. Nothing more."

"I need a break," Vance said.

"You need to stay focused, Vance," Howard said.

"I need a break," Vance repeated, walking toward the back entrance. "Ten minutes."

"Five minutes," Howard said. "And come back ready to play."

Vance gave Howard a thumbs up and walked out. Vinny was glad Howard didn't push his brother. You could only get so much out of Vance before he needed to recharge…and smoke.

"Can I eat lunch?" Brad asked.

"After you show me a hundred perfect paradiddles," Howard said. "*Perfect* paradiddles. No slop-slop."

Brad picked up his sticks. Vinny followed his brother outside.

Brilliant sunlight made the back patio an oasis after the dark confines of the studio. Vinny shaded his eyes. Vance sat on a concrete bench, legs crossed beneath him, hands over his ears. Their parents sat in Adirondack chairs a few feet away, beside a fire pit, a wishing well, and a trellis adorned with a string of lights.

Peggy and Rich basked in sunlight, the skin on their cheeks and foreheads red. Vinny needed to move Mom and Dad around like potted plants, keep them watered and out of direct sun so they didn't dry out. Pegdick appeared fine other than mild sunburn and small, X-shaped scars near the base of their skulls. Vinny wasn't sure if Howard Phillips sewed something inside their heads, or if the shape itself worked the resurrection. Peggy and Rich were no longer junkies. They were no longer anything but empty vessels awaiting orders. Vinny liked his parents so much better now.

"How are you crazy kids doing?" Vinny asked. His parents looked at him in blank-stared unison.

"Fine, Vincent," Peggy said. "How's rehearsal?"

"Great, Peg. How about you and Dad go inside and wipe down the equipment. Get out of the sun. You're burning up out here."

"Okay, son," Peggy said. His parents didn't exactly shamble back into the studio, but they took baby steps, as if unsure of their footing.

Vinny crouched before his brother and mimed putting on headphones. Vance shook his head. Vinny lit a cigarette, took a drag, and placed it between his brother's lips. Vance closed his eyes and took a few puffs. A minute later he uncovered his ears. Vinny lit another smoke and sat down next to his brother.

"All quiet now," Vinny said. "You good?"

Vance didn't reply.

"Howie's on fire today," Vinny said. "Brad has him vexed, but I'm not sure why. Guy's a decent drummer."

"Howard's an asshole," Vance said.

"True," Vinny replied. "His bowels are especially irritable today."

"Why is he driving us so hard anyway?" Vance asked.

Vinny didn't know. It wasn't like they had gigs booked. Howard Phillips planned to hire a drummer and put them on tour, but for the past month all they did was audition percussionists and rehearse strange classical music. *What kind of band is this?* Six weeks ago, when Howard kicked back in Dad's recliner in the living room and laid out his master plan—their reanimated parents quietly preparing breakfast in the kitchen—Vinny imagined being in a pre-packaged boy band, the next One Direction. But it was shaping up to be the next Kronos Quartet, or something even more bizarre.

"Whatever. We're getting paid," Vinny replied. "Howard took care of Pegdick's mortgage, so the house is safe."

"Yeah, but *why* is he paying us? For what?" Vance asked. "Record companies don't come along and pay off your mortgage, Vinny. Something is up."

"Howie has delivered everything he said he would. He brought Pegdick back, for Christ's sake!" Vinny said. "What else can we do but go along? What other options do we have?"

Vance tossed his smoke to the ground and crushed it beneath his heel. Vinny considered it a micro-aggression since there was an ashtray right next to the bench.

"There are always other options, Mr. Flip-Flop," Vance said. "Six weeks ago you wanted to have Howard Phillips arrested. Now you're ready to blow him."

"Six weeks ago we were in deep shit and Mr. Phillips bailed us out, just like you said he would," Vinny replied. "Trust yourself, Vance. It's okay. We're going to be okay."

Vance let out a deep sigh. He looked sallow and gaunt, skin draped loosely over a skull.

"You taking your medicine, Van?" Vinny asked.

"Yes, I've taking my damn medicine!" Vance spat. "Shit sucks. I can't sleep and it gives me headaches."

"The doctor said you need to give it a few weeks to kick-in," Vinny said. "Hang in there."

"Fuck the doctor, too!" Vance said.

"Consider him fucked," Vinny replied.

Vance put his face in his hands.

"Want me to see if Howie will give us the afternoon off?" Vinny asked.

"He'll never do that."

"Fuck him. If you're sick, you're sick, Van."

"I'm not sick! I'm fine!"

"Sounds like it," Vinny said. "Keep doing what you're doing, bro. You're doing good."

They sat in silence. Vinny finished his smoke and Vance lit another. Vinny sang the first verse of "Yesterday." Vance joined him on the chorus and took the second verse on his own.

"*Suddenly...I'm not half the man I used to be...*" Vance sang, though he sounded like twice the man he was moments earlier, his voice strong and clear. When the song was through, Vinny stood.

"Come on, bro," he said. "Let's go rock the Howie way. Hopefully Brad is done paradiddling."

Brad finished his paradiddles, but not his lunch. He quickly stuffed the rest of his sandwich into his mouth and took a seat behind the drum set. He looked tired and scared, slowly chewing the wadded food in his puffed-out cheeks.

Pegdick set up new equipment and packed away the old. A six-string electric bass replaced Vinny's viola and a rack of synthesizers hovered next to Vance's piano. Peggy and Rich diligently polished the drum cymbals until Howard Phillips shooed them away and told them to stand in a corner.

"This is our afternoon project," Howard said, handing out grainy photocopies of sheet music. "The three pages I've given you are part of a much larger musical work, a very old and timeless piece of music. It's so old, in fact, that complete notation of the song no longer exists, only fragments and scraps that have been compiled over the years. But it's enough to get you started."

Vance spread the sheets out on the piano. "Why is the second page different?" he asked.

Vinny hadn't noticed at first, but the second photocopy

looked even older than the first, as if the source material were a stone tablet or a picture on a cave wall. The staff contained an odd assortment of lines, slashes, and dots, and it took Vinny a minute to figure out what notes were being depicted. Once he did, his head began to ache and his heart raced.

"I don't like this," Brad said aloud, echoing Vinny's thoughts. Vinny was impressed Brad could read music notation beyond drum charts. "This is...not good."

Howard Phillips ignored Brad.

"You're very perceptive, Vance," Howard said. "The second page *does* come from a different source. But, I assure you, these three pages represent one continuous piece of music."

"Looks...very strange," Vance said, studying the pages.

"Crazy," Vinny added.

"I don't want to play this," Brad declared. "This song is messed up. Can't we go back to Brahms?"

"No, we can't go back to *Brahms*!" Howard hissed. "This isn't about what you want or don't want. This is about performing a new piece of music with the same feeling and precision you put *into* playing Brahms. But, no, we can't go *back* to Brahms. There's no going *back to Brahms!*"

"But this music is..." Brad struggled to find a word that made sense of the nightmarish notes on the page. The best he could come up with was, "Bad. This is really, *really* bad."

"The only thing that's really, *really* bad is your attitude, Brad," Howard said. "That and your snare work. And your kick drum. And your overall sense of timing. Let's face it, Brad, you're a myriad of bad and if you'd like to keep your job, I'd suggest you play the piece...as written."

After a long pause, Brad shrunk behind the drum kit and

launched into a beat. The opening notes blossomed on the piano and Vinny struggled to keep up with his brother. The six-string bass was cumbersome, the neck as thick as a log, and the bass line bumped and ground against Vance's piano motif until it sounded like the instruments were at war, the chugging breath of battle-worn, shell-shocked soldiers marching through cratered fields of endless death.

The music swelled and swelled again. Vance found order among the chaos of notes and Vinny followed his lead. Brad fought to keep pace. The room grew hot, the air shimmered. Vinny felt headrush-dizzy. He spread his feet to reclaim his balance, but the room spun, and his fingers moved along the bass neck of their own accord. He looked up and the ceiling disappeared into swirling, living darkness. The walls oozed black slime. A blue mist hovered above the ground. It rolled over Vinny's shoes, as cold as ice.

"Fuck!" Brad stopped playing and jumped up from behind the drum kit, trying to climb atop the tiny stool. It reminded Vinny of elephants, mice, and circus tricks.

"Fuck! Shit! Fuck!" Brad said. Vinny and Vance stopped playing in unison.

"Mr. Thomas, please tell me why you are interrupting band rehearsal with your girlish scream?" Howard asked.

"Something crawled across my feet!" Brad said. "*Both* of my feet! Something *slithered* across them! Look, my shoes are wet!" Brad tried to lift his foot up to his face, but his oversized belly made it difficult. "Argh! They stink, too!"

"A professional musician can handle any situation and play through it." Howard sounded exhausted. "You *never* stop playing! The show must go on."

"This is insane!" Brad said. He picked his backpack and jacket off the floor, smelling the items first before deeming them safe to wear. "I'm leaving!"

"Perhaps that's for the best," Howard said. "Your brother Thomas can fill in on percussion."

Brad stopped in the middle of putting on his jacket. It looked like his arms were handcuffed behind his back.

"You'll never get my brother in here," Brad said. "He's too fat."

"I've already contacted Thomas," Howard said. "I hoped he could give you a few technical pointers, but it appears that won't be necessary. Your brother can play the parts himself."

"You can't fire me," Brad said, sounding unsure. "I have a contract with Arkham Records. It's got William Deacon Jr's signature on it!"

"So do a lot of people," Howard said. "I'm sure you will be re-assigned to a more appropriate role within the organization. Perhaps something more…sacrificial."

"You can't do this!" Brad shouted. "You can't replace me with my brother. He's too fat! It's not fair!"

"I'm afraid you're wrong on both counts, Brad," Howard said. "I'm going to have to ask you to leave now."

"How fat *is* your brother?" Vinny asked.

"Enormous," Brad said.

"And his name is Thomas?" Vance asked. "So your parents named him Thomas Thomas?"

"Yes."

"Are your parents assholes?"

"Sure," Brad said. "Aren't yours?"

Vance glanced at Peggy and Rich standing complacently in the corner, staring at the wall. Vinny was reminded of the final frames of *The Blair Witch Project*.

"Not anymore," Vance said.

"You've wasted enough of our rehearsal time already, Brad," Howard said. "Please go."

"Okay, okay. Listen, I'll chill out and play," Brad said, trying to convince both Howard and himself. "I'm sorry I freaked out. I got…that song…it's *evil*, man!"

"That song, and pieces like it, are Arkham Records' bread and butter…at least for the artists *I* manage," Howard said. "I'm sorry to say you are no longer on that roster, Brad. I need you to leave."

"Hey, I'm sorry!" Brad said. "I just…I got the willies. Let me try again."

"No, thank you, Brad," Howard said. He summoned Pegdick with a curt wave. "Please, show Mr. Thomas the door."

Mom nodded. She crossed the studio quicker than Vinny expected. She grabbed Brad by the arm, Dad right behind her.

"Stop!" Brad cried. "That hurts!"

Dad grabbed Brad's other arm and pulled him toward the door. Brad resisted and Dad gave him a head-butt that rocked Brad back on his heels. Dad continued to batter Brad with his forehead. Mom could only reach Brad's shoulders, but she got in a solid throat shot that buckled Brad's knees and silenced his protests. They hoisted Brad outside and the door swung shut behind them.

"That was harsh, don't you think, Mr. Phillips?" Vance looked sheepish and jumpy. He needed a cigarette. Vinny, too. They needed to get out of the dark studio and back into the sunlight. Vinny was briefly jealous of Brad. *Will Pegdick beat him all the way to his car?*

"Yes, it was harsh," Howard said. "But it was necessary. There is no time to waste with musicians who lack the drive or talent to see our mission through to completion. Prune the dead wood quickly. It allows for new growth."

"What exactly *is* our mission. Mr. Phillips?" Vinny asked. He pointed to the sheet music using his middle finger. "And what is *that* we played?"

Howard rubbed his temples.

"An old song," Howard said. "And our mission is to put a band together to play it. It shouldn't be this hard. Brad was a poor choice. His brother is our man."

CHAPTER THREE
Bang On The Drum

Thom Thomas was more than fat. He was the most enormous person Vinny ever saw. He didn't even look human, his basketball-sized head sitting atop a mountain of flesh like a meatball atop a pile of spaghetti. Thomas had legs the size of tree trunks, arms that stuck out like logs from his massive, gelatinous torso. His belly hung to his knees, draped to the floor when he sat.

Peggy and Rich transported Thom Thomas into the rehearsal studio on a heavy-duty John Deere utility vehicle. They drove in through the garage door and took Thom directly to the drum kit. It took twenty minutes to get Thomas off the vehicle and onto the steel chair behind the kit. His massive bulk dwarfed the drum set as if it were a child's toy. Peggy set up an oxygen tank and mask next to Thom's floor tom and Thom spent the next several minutes sucking oxygen, sounding like Darth Vadar.

"You're kidding, right?" Vance asked.

"How are we gonna tour?" Vinny asked, imagining Thom Thomas poured into the bed of a cargo truck.

"Leave your worries to me, boys," Howard said. "Say hello to your new drummer, Mr. Thom Thomas!"

The massive mound of flesh behind the drum kit waved a log-sized arm.

"Vance," Vance called out.

"Vinny," Vinny said.

Thom Thomas gulped oxygen for several moments before unstrapping his face mask.

"I'm Thom," he said. "I've heard a lot about you guys. Great playing with you."

"You've heard a lot about us from who?" Vance asked. Vinny mentally corrected the statement to end in "whom."

"Word gets around," Thom said. "I hear you guys are the best."

"According to whom?" Vinny asked. "Your douchebag brother?"

"Howard Phillips thinks very highly of you," Thom said. "I heard your mom and dad beat up my douchebag brother."

"It's true," Vinny said. "Pegdick kick ass."

"They haul ass too," Thomas said. "And I have a lot of ass to haul."

"How did you get to be so…big?" Vance asked.

"Years of intense overeating," Thom said. "You don't develop a striking figure like mine overnight. It takes years of dedication."

"I suppose so," Vinny said. "Congratulations."

"My body is a bloated pile of garbage," Thom said. "The Deacons say they'll get me into a new vessel when all this is all over. Before you know it, I'll be as skinny and good-looking as you guys."

"Who were the Deacons?" Vinny asked.

"William Deacon Jr. and William Deacon Sr.? Owners of Arkham Records? The guys who sign your paychecks?" Thom asked. The names meant nothing to Vinny. He had direct deposit.

"And the Deacons are going to get you a new…vessel?" Vance asked.

"Yeah, I need to get out of this thing," Thom sad, lifting his arms and making the hanging waddles of flesh dance. "I'm a disgusting mess."

"Can't argue with you there," Vance said.

"You could get your stomach stapled," Vinny suggested. "Or, like, go on a diet."

"Yeah," Thom replied. "Fuck that."

Vance stepped close to Howard Phillips, speaking low so only Howard and Vinny could hear.

"Can he travel?" Vance asked. "We're supposed to tour with this guy, right?"

Vance and Vinny stared at Thom Thomas as if he were a great, lumbering, zoo-beast. Vinny wasn't sure if he should take a selfie with Thom or toss him peanuts.

"I told you already, leave the travel and touring arrangements to me," Howard said. "While Mr. Thomas does have some physical issues that limit his mobility, I assure you, gentlemen, you will never find a more graceful or adept individual behind a drum kit."

Howard handed out sheet music, the same strange song that upset Brad last rehearsal.

"I'm sure the Boyles will recall this little ditty. How about running through it half-time to get Thom up to speed?"

Thom Thomas didn't need much time to get up to speed. He got the beat running and never stopped, switching it around, swapping time signatures, adding earsplitting, head-rattling drum fills at every opportunity. Vinny found his style too flashy, but there was no denying the guy's skills.

By the time they reached the top of page two, the air swirled with spirits, fantastic, there-and-gone creatures that shimmered in the air, wet-dry, smooth-spiked, blink-and-you-miss-it flashes of fur and fangs, scales and claws, black eyes and open mouths, and teeth, teeth, teeth. Everywhere Vinny looked, another sharp, otherworldly smile greeted him.

Vance's expression was neutral, placid, his fingers flying over the keyboards, one hand on the piano, the other hammering the synthesizer. *Did he still follow the sheet music?* Vinny squinted at the page, but the notes danced and jittered. He blinked twice but it didn't help. They'd reached the point in the song where Vinny's hands and fingers switched to autopilot and his soul stirred like it was lifting out of his body.

Thom Thomas never missed a beat, smiling from ear-to-ear, his massive face glowing like a sweaty, red, jack-o-lantern. He looked ready to burst. *At least he'll die happy,* Vinny thought.

The end of page three couldn't come soon enough. Vinny stared at his shoes so he wouldn't have to look at Thom's orgasmic expression, his brother's vacant stare, or the impossible, swimming horrors that filled the rehearsal studio. The floor offered no comfort. A spiraling black hole formed in the middle of the room, and the monster-mist swirled around it like a whirlpool, everything getting sucked down into deep, bottomless black.

Vinny closed his eyes and one of the creatures brushed past his face, ruffling his long, dishwater hair. Its touch felt light as a feather, rubbery, and live-dead. Vinny's stomach cramped, but the song came to an end before he puked all over his floor pedals.

Howard Phillips applauded.

"Very nice for a first time, boys!" he said. "I like what I'm seeing...and hearing!"

"Uh...I think I'm going to be sick," Vinny said, gingerly

removing his bass and placing it on the stand. The room spun even though the smoke and monsters faded with the music. "That song is…," a replay of Brad's meltdown flashed across Vinny's mind before he chose his next word, "…*intense*."

"It is if you play it right, Vincent," Howard said. "And you boys did a magnificent job, I must say. A few tweaks here and there and you'll be ready to hit the road."

"What are …" *those awful creatures?* Vinny wanted to ask. "What is that song? What's it called?"

"It's a very old song that's been in the Arkham library for a long time," Howard said. "The Deacons want it revived, given a modern twist, and you young men are just the musicians to do it. The song has many names. Musicians have called it—"

"The Infinitus! *Woo-hoo*!" Thom Thomas raised his massive arms in the air, his voice high and girlish. "Fantastic! I've read about it and seen video, but I've never been *in the room* during the Infinitus … never been *part* of a Summoning Ceremony!" He looked eagerly at Vinny and Vance. "What level wizards are you? You must be, like, sixes or sevens to play like that. No underclassman could perform the ritual with such precision. How long have you studied Nyarlathotep? Are you in Noden's class?"

"'The Wizard!" Vance shouted, launching into a cover of the Black Sabbath tune on the synthesizer. Thom looked puzzled.

"Fuck's fat boy talking about, Howard?" Vinny asked, shouting to be heard over his brother's playing. Howard shot him an icy look.

"Ah, Peg? Richard?" Howard called. Vinny's parents were on the floor in the corner, bent into bizarre yoga-like shapes. Richard looked like a crab, his head twisted almost completely around, staring down the length of his back through the bridge of his arms and legs.

"Jesus Christ!" Vinny shouted. "What the hell is wrong with them?"

"It's the music," Howard said dismissively, as Vinny's parents slowly unraveled themselves and stood upright. "It inspires some individuals to…assume positions associated with…certain musical ceremonies…very ancient rites… It means you're playing the song right, Vincent. No worries."

"You speak in riddles, Howard. It's annoying," Vinny said. His stomach lurched and he wondered if vomiting on Howard would emphasize his point or hurt his argument. "What's Thom talking about? Why are my parents twisted up like pretzels?"

"Give me a moment and I'll explain," Howard said. "Peg? Rich? Can you extract Mr. Thomas from the drum kit and get him lunch, please? I think that last performance earned us all an early break, no?"

"I don't need to eat. I can keep playing," Thom said, slipping the oxygen mask over his face and gulping air. Pegdick stood behind him, waiting to help him stand. Howard ignored Thom.

"Why don't you step outside, Vincent?" Howard said. "Fresh air and sunshine will make you feel better." *I must look as bad as I feel*, Vinny thought.

"I'm going to smoke," Vance said, heading for the studio door.

"Me too," Vinny said. "Come with us, Mr. Phillips."

"I don't smoke."

"Come out and get some fresh air," Vinny said.

"I hardly see how you can call the air 'fresh,' if you're polluting it with your cigarette smoke," Howard said.

"Some sun then," Vinny said.

"Sunlight is overrated. History is made at night," Howard said. "But I'll come."

Howard followed the Boyle brothers out to the patio. It was overcast, sticky, and humid, but Vinny was still relieved to be out of the studio.

"Where did Big Boy go to school?" Vance asked after lighting a Marlboro. "Hogwarts Academy? Or has he graduated to old Miskatonic U?"

"Thomas was home-schooled," Howard said. "Just because he has an educational background or belief system different from your own is no reason to mock him, Vance. Obviously his size prevented him from attending traditional schools. It's also made him painfully shy and more than a little lacking in social skills. Can you give the man a break? He's got a drive and determination that belies his somewhat unconventional appearance. He'll serve you well as the band progresses."

"What are we progressing *toward*?" Vinny asked. The horrors he'd experienced inside the studio a few minutes prior seemed impossible beneath the light of day. Had he imagined the whole thing?

"He wants us to play Lovecraft songs," Vance said. "What is it we're playing? The music of Erich Zann?"

"Who the hell is Erich Zann?" Vinny asked, wondering if his brother was tossing another word salad. *Miskatonic U*? Howard's eyes narrowed as he studied Vance.

"Zann is credited with the first page of the piece," Howard said. "A musician named Sonny Deacon wrote the third page. He founded Arkham Records and Recording. The author of the second page is unknown, but it dates back several millennia, somewhere between 220 and 185 B.C."

"So it's a compilation of different songs arranged to make a new piece?" Vinny asked, lighting a cigarette.

"No. It's the same song," Howard said.

"How can three different musicians, in three different

time periods, write the same song?" Vinny asked.

Instead of answering, Howard turned to Vance.

"Do you understand what we're doing, Vance?" Howard asked. "The importance of our work?"

"I think so," Vance said.

"Good. Can you explain it to your brother?" Howard asked. "I can't stay out here much longer with you two human smoke machines. It's disgusting."

Vinny and Vance blew smoke directly into Howard's face. He gagged and backed away, flapping his arms in front of him.

"Assholes," Howard muttered, retreating back inside the studio.

"What are we playing?" Vinny asked.

"I don't know," Vance answered.

"You just told Howie you did!"

"I don't know," Vance repeated, chain-smoking another cigarette. "It's weird..."

"Damn right, it's weird," Vinny said. "Who is Erich Zann? Is he the actor from *Titanic*?"

"No, bonehead," Vance said. "Do you know who H.P. Lovecraft is?"

"The horror writer? Isn't he dead?"

"He died in the 1930s," Vance said. "He wrote a story about a student named Erich Zann who lived next door to a blind viola player whose music opened a doorway to another dimension. Well, a window, actually."

"But that shit's *fiction*, right?" Vinny asked.

"I thought so," Vance shrugged. "But now...well, you've heard the song. You've seen what it does."

"What does it do?" Vinny asked. "Open a doorway to another dimension?"

"Well, a window, actually," Vance corrected.

"Vance, are those creatures...the monsters in the

mist…are they from…outer space?" Vinny couldn't believe he even asked such a ridiculous question, but followed it up with an even sillier query. "Are the monsters *drawn* to the song or do they live *inside* the song?"

"I don't know," Vance said again. "I think the song is attracting *something*. Monsters, maybe. Hopefully a monster-sized audience. It's a groovy tune."

"Is it dangerous, Vance?" Vinny asked. "Those things are so…horrible."

"They look strange, but I don't think they'll hurt us as long as we're playing," Vance said.

"One banged into my head, today, bro!" Vinny said. "Those fucking things are *gross*!"

"They're okay," Vance said.

"Don't they scare the shit out of you?" Vinny asked.

"I'm schizophrenic, Vin," Vance replied. "I see scary stuff all the time." He waited a moment before adding, "No, I'm not afraid, Vinny. I think the music is helping me."

"You're still taking—"

"Yes, yes, I'm still taking my meds. But I think the music is helping me more. Maybe this song is my new 'Yesterday,' you know?"

"Well, if it's good for you, it's good for me, Van," Vinny said, though he dreaded returning to the studio to play the song again.

"Another thing," Vance said, standing and walking toward the studio door. "The H.P. in H.P. Lovecraft stands for Howard Phillips."

"No shit? Do you think *our* Howard Phillips is *the* Howard Phillips? The same guy?" Vinny asked. "Should we check the back of his head for one of those x-shaped scar thingies like Mom and Dad have?"

"No, I don't think he's…like Mom and Dad," Vance

said. "He's something else. I...I don't know what exactly. Come on. Let's go play before Big Thom bursts."

Vinny told his brother to go ahead and lit another cigarette. He was in no hurry to get back. *That song demands sacrifice*, Vinny thought, wondering how much more he and Vance had left to give.

CHAPTER FOUR
March Of The Pigs

"Okay, boys. Tonight's sacrifice is pinkie toes," Howard said. "Off with your shoes and socks and pony up."

The tiny dressing room of The Boom-Boom Room in Kalamazoo, MI smelled faintly of urine, both human and animal. Thom Thomas was wedged into a corner. It must've taken a gallon of lube and a plunger to get him in there. Pegdick helped him take off his shoes.

"I lost both my pinkie toes two years ago," Thom told Howard. "Diabetes."

"Well, we'll take the next toe over…or whatever's left down there," Howard said, watching Peggy gingerly handle Thom's football-shaped foot. "It's the thought that counts, Thom…and the blood sacrifice."

The blood sacrifices ratcheted up over the past two months, as their Endless Tour followed the Mississippi from Canada to New Orleans. Vinny couldn't figure out how Howard planned the tour, apparently using geological formations and weather patterns to book shows rather than audience interest or venue location. The band played a lot of strange places during the past year. A Hopi reservation, the median of a highway in Manitoba, and an upscale living room packed with people wearing ball gowns, tuxedos, and Guy Fawkes masks, to name a few. At least The Boom-Boom Room had a dressing room and a stage.

They played under a variety of names: The Heartache Trio, The Heart Attack Trio, The Big Hands Trio, Blizzard, Flurry, Big Mac and The Shoe-Strings. (Vinny's favorite moniker was Our Drummer's Morbidly Obese, but Howard hated how it looked on the marquee.) "The Summoning Song," as Vinny and Vance called it (Thom insisted on calling it "The Infinitus," squealing like a schoolgirl every time he said it), was always the centerpiece of their set. They played other songs, a mix of jazz standards, oddball covers, and a growing list of original numbers. Vance's "Lucille Sounds Funny Tonight" paid tribute to blues great B.B. King, with Vance switching between violin and saxophone, while "Collie Flower Stew" was a brooding mediation for viola and piano that channeled the spirits of Cole Porter, Charles Mingus, and Iron Maiden.

Vinny loved the way the band branched out musically, and life on the road had a fun, class-trip vibe. But Vance grew sullen around the middle of Florida. Vinny feared the rigors of the road and the blood sacrifices were too much for Vance. He played wonderfully during shows—and was blissfully unaffected by the flying, otherworldly monsters that appeared wherever they played—but before and after performances, Vance looked pale and sickly. Vinny didn't ask his brother if he took his meds. Instead he waited until Vance was asleep and counted the pills in the bottle. Vance took his meds.

"Perky, please fetch our Offering Chamber so we can make our donations and get the show started," Howard ordered.

Peter 'Perky' Perkins joined the crew late last year, quitting his job as a strip club bouncer in Nagadoches, TX, and joining the tour along with his girlfriend, a dancer named Becky. The Offering Chamber—a 10-gallon plastic Rubbermaid storage bin (with new, improved, airtight locking lid)—contained the remains of previous sacrifices. A reddish-brown soup sloshed around the bottom of the container, seasoned with fingernails, burnt hair, skin scrappings, old scabs, the bones of a humming bird, the pelt of a dead dog, the head of a stray cat, and not-so-fresh roadkill. Perky dragged the plastic bin across the dressing room floor. A yellow, feline eye stared accusingly at Vinny before tumble-floating away in the jostling waves. Perky peeled off the lid, turning his head to avoid the smell, but it was no use. The stench permeated the room instantly, making everyone gag except for Peggy and Richard. Judging from the way Peggy cuddled Thom's sweaty foot, Vinny guessed his mother had lost her sense of smell.

"The Offering Chamber is pretty ripe, Howard," Vance said. "Can we empty and clean it?"

"We can and we shall…the next time the moon is full and we're near running water, according to protocol," Howard said, covering his nose and mouth with a monogrammed handkerchief. "Meanwhile, let's get our sacrifices done so we can literally close the lid on the Offering Chamber and get on with tonight's performance. Chop-chop! Snip-snip! Peggy, will you help Thomas begin tonight's ceremony."

Peggy Boyle used pruning shears to chop off the middle toe on Thom's bloated foot.

"Ouch! Ouch! It hurts!" Thom screamed until Peggy slathered a bluish cream on his bloody stump, which appeared to both seal and soothe the wound.

"Ah…better," Thom said. "Anything for The Infinitus, Mr. Phillips."

Peggy picked Thom's severed toe off the floor and

tossed it into the Offering Chamber with a plop.

"Very good," Howard said, quietly reciting a phrase in Latin, or some other jibber-jabber language. Every ceremony was the same, but Vinny still didn't know what Howard was saying. "Vance? Would you care to go next?"

"Sure. I got this, Ma," Vance said. He took the pruning shears from his mother and opened the jaws wide, placing the blades between his pinkie toe and the toe beside it. He glanced at Vinny. For reassurance? Guidance? Support? Vinny didn't know. Vance slammed the shears closed with a click, and his tiny toe tumbled through the air, hitting the rim of the Offering Chamber before bouncing to the floor. Vance grunted. Vinny wasn't sure if it was from pain or disappointment his shot missed. Vance dropped the shears and grabbed his foot, blood spurting from the stub. Mom greased his toe with magic blue slime until the pain subsided. Wee, wee, wee, all the way home, Vance.

"Damn, Howard," Vance said, rolling his sock back onto his foot. "How many more blood sacrifices do we need to make? If we start lopping off fingers we won't be able to play. And I think I can speak for my brother when I say we both like being able to walk, and toes really help us keep our balance. Thom doesn't walk anyway…can't you take two extra toes from him and let us keep ours?"

"You know that's not how it works, Vance. Everybody needs to contribute a little something," Howard said. He picked Vance's toe off the floor and tossed it into the Offering Chamber, muttering the same strange incantation as before. Then he took the pruning shears, wiped them clean with his monogrammed handkerchief, and handed them to Vinny. The handles were still sticky, and left pink residue on Vinny's palms. "Your turn, Vincent."

"Do the guys in Greta Van Fleet have to chop their toes off, too?" Vinny's left shoe was off, but he took his time rolling down his sock.

"I have it on good authority Greta Van Fleet's record label made them cut off their *balls*," Howard smiled. "Same for Maroon 5. Consider yourself fortunate, Vincent."

Vinny slipped the shears around his pinkie toe and squeezed. Pain shot up his leg. Every fiber of his being screamed for him to stop.

"I can't do this," Vinny said.

"Sure you can, Vincent," Howard said. "Richard, please help your son remove his toe so we can get started."

Vinny's Dad started to cross the room, but Perky was faster. He snatched the shears from Vinny's hand.

"I'll do it," Perky said. He cupped Vinny's heel and lifted his leg straight up, making Vinny pinwheel his arms and fall backwards. Before Vinny could regain his balance, Perky switched his grip to Vinny's pinkie toe, quickly snipping the digit off with the shears. He tossed Vinny's toe into the sacrificial soup.

"Fuck, Pete!" Vinny shouted. "Fuck this! Fuck you! Fuck *all* of you! This is crazy Satan-worshipping bullshit!"

Vinny screamed profanities until his mother covered his bloody foot with salve. After a momentary burning sensation, the pain vanished. The blue slime smelled slightly minty and medicinal. It reminded Vinny of Vicks Vape-o-Rub.

"There, there now, Vincent," Howard said. "Quiet down and put your big boy pants on."

"What is this stuff?" Vinny pointed to his foot.

"A homeopathic remedy from Dr. Corba," Howard said. "It's old medicine. Good medicine."

"Will it make our toes grow back?" Vance asked. Thom seemed interested, probably hoping his diabetes digits might regenerate.

"If you believe hard enough, Vance, anything can happen," Howard answered. "Now let's get you boys on stage. The show must go on."

"How come *you* don't cut anything off for the O Chamber?" Vinny asked, watching Howard mutter words over the plastic container, toss in a pinch of powder, and step back so Perky could reseal the plastic lid. *Don't forget to burp it, Perk!*

"First, I'm not a member of the band. I'm your manager," Howard said. "Second, my sacrifices may not be visible, but they are as real and as great as your own, I assure you."

"Can I count your fingers and toes to make sure?" Vance asked.

"Start with this one," Howard said, flipping Vance the bird. "We've got ten minutes until showtime. Peter and I will secure the Offering Chamber. I suggest you boys do your pre-show prep. I advise finger stretches and vocal warm-ups, though I'm sure the Boyle brothers will opt for their usual chain-smoking session. Wise up, boys. You only get one set of lungs."

"Perk! Tell Becky I need a blowjob before we go on," Thom called out and silence fell over the room. Peter Perkins nodded sheepishly and dragged the Offering Chamber into the corner. Vinny frowned at Thom. They all dropped loads in Becky, but there was an unspoken rule about not cuckolding Perky. Fuck Thom and his lack of social skills!

"I need to get my nut," Thom said by way of explanation, but it did nothing to ease the awkward tension. The thought of little Becky navigating rolls of Thom's fat in search of his erection made Vinny's stomach flip.

Dressing room weirdness aside, the show rocked.

"Lucille" cooked and "Collie Flower" steamed. "The Summoning Song" went on for nearly twenty minutes, a giant vortex swirling in the middle of the Boom-Boom Room's dance floor. A creature emerged from the vortex with a shower of sparks and a flash of flame. Its body was the size of a German Shepherd, but its leathery wings spanned twelve feet tip-to-tip. It batted its wings, pelting Vinny with droplets of foul-smelling liquid.

The creature circled the Boom-Boom Room, breathing fire on the audience. Dozens of people danced around the club, engulfed in flames like Hollywood stuntmen, only no one rushed in from the wings with fire extinguishers and safety blankets to put them out. The flaming dancers stopped, dropped, and rolled into the gaping black hole in the middle of the floor, or danced until they fell into smoldering, smoking heaps. The flying nightmare swooped in, feasting on the roasted flesh of the fallen.

The band played until the ceiling caught fire and the emergency sprinklers threatened to douse their equipment. Firemen broke through the blacked-out windows with double-headed axes. The band broke down in record time, everybody grabbing gear and hauling it outside. Even Becky carried a saxophone case in one hand and Thom's snare drum in the other. The last thing left on stage was Thom Thomas, sitting in a puddle of sprinkler water on his steel-reinforced drum throne. Richard rolled in with the John Deere a minute later, and hauled him out with the help of Peggy and Perk.

"Good show tonight, gentlemen," Howard said, overseeing the load-out in the parking lot of the Boom-Boom Room.

"Cool dragon!" Thom said. Richard used a small forklift to hoist Thom into his modified transit van. "Way cooler than that shitty cockroach-thing we got in Albuquerque, right?"

The Albuquerque show (Offering: two-inch strips of skin torn from the middle of their backs—Perky used a potato peeler) featured a flurry of flying squid and one-eyed creatures with impossibly long teeth. The dance floor vortex belched up a three-foot-long dung beetle. The enormous insect scurried twice around the swirling black hole before it rolled over on its back and died.

Vinny and Vance followed Howard, Perky, and Becky onto the tour bus. Peggy and Richard followed behind in the transit van with Thom. Vance said Thom needed to sleep sitting up so the fat around his neck didn't crush his windpipe, but Vinny wasn't sure if it was true. Vance had strange beliefs and an active imagination.

"Why do our fans have to die?" Vance asked. The hopelessness in his voice worried Vinny and caught Howard's attention.

"Not everyone dies, Vance. Your parents are still with us," Howard said. When he saw that wasn't the answer Vance needed, Howard added, "Some songs demand sacrifice."

"I can't take much more...or give much more," Vance said. "We're killing people. We're murderers. We have to stop."

"Pretend it's a video game, Van," Vinny said. Getting lost in the music made it easy. "That's what I do."

"It's not *pretend*, Vinny," Vance said. "People are dead because of us. We're killing people!"

"You're not murderers," Howard cut in. "You're musicians. If people choose to sacrifice themselves to the music you create, that is their choice. They're happy to do it, Vance. Every show draws bigger and bigger crowds. People have heard about what you're accomplishing and want to experience it for themselves. They're willing to give themselves entirely to your music. You should be flattered, Vance."

"Why does our music make people kill themselves?" Vance asked. "It's like the Hungarian suicide song."

"Perhaps there's a link," Howard said. "But the song you're performing is much older and more important. The sacrifices are necessary for what is to come and it's a cause your fans are happy to give their lives for."

"You think those people were happy being flamed-roasted and eaten by a dragon tonight?"

"Yes, I do," Howard said. "Sure, there's the occasional barfly or security guard who gets caught in the mosh, but, for the most part, your fans are eager to experience your music and all it demands. Your fans would die for you."

"I don't want them to." Vance sounded like a small child. Howard treated him like one.

"It's not your place to worry, Vance. Your job is to play," Howard said. "You do it beautifully. Both of you. Enjoy it. Have fun. Go forth and make a joyful noise. You're doing the Lord's work."

"What Lord?" Vinny asked, but Howard only smiled. *Damn, he's got a mouth like a shark.*

"I thought the song helped me more than the meds," Vance said. "But the side effects are terrible."

"The price of the performing arts is our very souls, Mr. Boyle," Howard said. "You boys played a magnificent show tonight. That is all that is required of you. Rest now. Tomorrow we'll get back to conquering the world."

Vance nodded. Vinny extended his hand and pulled his brother up. They shuffled to their tiny, two-bunk room at the back of the bus. Vance had a nosebleed. Vinny handed him a tissue.

"That song is stealing our souls," Vance said, tissue stuffed up his left nostril, head tilted back. He sat on his lower bunk and kicked off his shoes. "It gets under your skin and inside your head."

"Don't worry about your soles, bro," Vinny said. "We'll get you a new pair of shoes."

"This is serious, Vinny," Vance said.

"More serious than cutting off our toes?" Vinny asked. "More serious than a dragon roasting and eating our audience?"

"Yeah, it's bad…," Vance said, but his sentence ended in a snore. Vance literally fell asleep as soon as his head hit the pillow. He looked as gaunt and wasted as a junkie.

"Pretend it's a video game, bro," Vinny said softly, more to himself than to his brother. *Were there bonus lives? Special weapons? A reset button?* "Pretend it's a game."

CHAPTER FIVE
Traveling Man

They played a waterside venue called Barlow's Tavern and Tackle in Oak Harbor, WA under the name The Love Crafters. Vinny hated the name and worried the floor of Barlow's, which hung out over the harbor, wouldn't support the combined weight of the audience and Thom.

"Maybe Thom should stay on solid ground," Vinny suggested during soundcheck. "We can mike him and pipe his parts in through the PA."

"You worry too much, Vinny," Howard reassured him. "Barlow's Tavern has stood for a hundred years and will stand for a hundred more. If this place can survive the harsh winters of the Pacific Northwest, it can survive The Love Crafters!"

Howard was gloriously wrong. The band had zig-zagged across land-locked states for months, "The Summoning Song" percolating. As they got closer to the coast, the song gained momentum, drawing strength from the water, drawing bigger, more substantial nightmares to the shows. They played a lake community picnic outside Spokane last week and a giant turtle rose from the water, silently watching "The Summoning Song" from the beach, as transfixed by the strange music as the fans. The turtle stuck around until the end of the song, snapping the heads off two children standing by the water's edge before submerging, its webbed claws the size of rowboats. *How does it fit in the lake?* Vinny pondered, watching the bodies of the decapitated children bob on the rippling water. The band wrapped up with covers of Jeff Beck's "Freeway Jam" and The Beatles' "Love Me Do."

They launched into the opening run of "The Summoning Song" at Barlow's and the room filled with swirling spirits, creatures with long teeth, countless arms and legs, innumerable eyes, slowly patrolling the dance floor like robotic vacuums, touching and feeling everything in their paths. Water levels surged, the fishing villages and designer mansions along Rosario and Haro Straits washing away. Something huge and prehistoric swam up the Strait of Juan de Fuca and all the creatures in Skagit and Padilla Bays breached in unison, a great clash of flapping fins, helpless gills, and gashing teeth, hundreds of thousands of airborne fish (even two grey whales) hovered above the water for a terrified moment as an ancient threat from the deep invaded their home.

Fishermen as far north as Vancouver and as far south as Seattle claimed water zombies overran Cypress Island—flesh-eating monsters crawled out of the bay and cleared the island of every living soul in a matter of hours—but the rest of the world accepted the more palatable and plausible suggestion that the tiny island's population simply washed away. The freak storm brought waves as high as Barlow's windows, but none of the people in the crowded bar—mostly dark-eyed teenagers—appeared to care. The swirling black vortex returned and kids jumped in, some grabbing their knees as if diving cannonball-style into a swimming pool, some calmly stepping off and falling into the abyss, some dancing their way in, some diving head-first. Only a few got tossed in against their will.

Tears streamed down Vance's face. Vinny felt his brother's pain, but he couldn't stop playing. Once "The Summoning Song" started, you played it through until the end. That's what Howard claimed, but Vinny suspected he relayed orders from a higher authority. *The Deacons? Who did they answer to?* It didn't matter. There came a point when the song took over and practically played itself. At times, during these auto-pilot, body-snatching takeovers, Vinny wondered how much Howard and his bosses even needed him and his brother. If Howard had the ability to bring Peg and Rich back, maybe he could teach them to play "The Summoning Song" too. But Howard's power must fall short of that or Vinny and Vance would already be gone, given the "Brad goodbye," head-butted off the tour by Pegdick.

The only member of The Love Crafters enjoying himself was Thom. He happily slammed away behind the drum kit, smiling like a goon. Several people in the audience held signs reading, "Thom Thomas Is God," and "Bigfoot Warning: Thom Thomas In Da House!" A few people called out requests for "Lucille," and "Collie Flower Stew," which made Vinny happy…though many of those same people later twisted themselves into human pretzels and fell/hopped/rolled into the swirling black hole to nowhere.

The final chords faded, the wooden bones of Barlow's cracking beneath the freakish waves. Vance sat shaking behind his keyboards. Perky and Vinny dragged him off stage while Pegdick hoisted Thom back to the transit van.

"Was that him? Was it Cthulu? In the water?" Thom asked, more excited than Vinny had ever seen him. "I felt it! I felt his holy presence like a black fire inside me! Did you guys feel it? You felt it, right?"

Thom always wanted to chat after shows. It took Vinny several months before he realized Thom was locked in the van whenever he wasn't playing and this was his only opportunity to speak with other people. (Pegdick were good listeners, but didn't say much.) Vinny sympathized with Thom's loneliness and made an effort to spend more time with him outside of gigs. But he found Thom's lengthy dissertations on wizarding, the history of percussion, and the god-like powers of Howard Phillips exhausting.

Tonight wasn't a chat night. Vance puked at the bottom of the stage stairs, his nose bleeding again. Vinny and Perky helped him onto the bus, plopping him down on the sofa. Vinny fetched his brother two Xanax, a shot of tequila, and a joint. Perky left to finish breaking down the equipment. They'd picked up two more roadies in Utah— Blade and Gary—and the trio could clear a roomful of gear in a matter of minutes. The increased efficiency helped tonight. Vinny saw Barlow's Tavern and Tackle topple into the harbor as their bus pulled away. He wet a washcloth in the bathroom sink and laid it across Vance's forehead.

"Just breath, Van," Vinny said. "Smell the pizza, blow out the candles. Smell the pizza, blow out the candles. In and out, bro."

"Yeah…yeah," Vance said. "Ah…it hurts all over, Vin. From the inside out."

They were almost through the second verse of "Yesterday" when Howard Phillips barged in, his smile wide and predatory.

"Fantastic show, boys! Fantastic!" Howard said, oblivious to Vance's pained expression. "You leveled up tonight, graduated to a new, permanent name. From this point on, the band will be called The Dunwich Horrors!"

Vinny felt the name was only marginally better than The Love Crafters. The Horrors played the next night in a tiny Northern California town called Hoopa at a bar/restaurant called The Shaft. The glass floor of the dining room overlooked an abandoned mine shaft. The band set up in the far corner, near the kitchen doors. Based on the rinky-dink PA, Vinny got the impression The Shaft didn't book many live acts. The Dunwich Horrors might be the first. They were certainly the last.

"Why are we playing this backwoods dive?" Vance asked before the set. The answer became obvious once they hit "The Summoning Song." Hundreds of bat-like creatures emerged from the abandoned mine shaft, sticking to the bottom of the glass, pulsating and pulling, stark white with pink, gaping orifi in the middle. The glass shattered, shards sparkling like a thousand diamonds falling into the dark shaft. The bat-things swarmed in on stubby bone wings. The Horror fans in Hoopa liked the inclusion of a real black hole rather than an inter-dimensional vortex, jumping into the old mine shaft in groups of twos and threes, laughing with mad joy the whole way down.

Thousands of yellow eyes surrounded The Shaft—indeed, the entire town of Hoopa—creatures that spent their entire lives in shadow, away from the eyes of man, yet couldn't resist the primal call of the song. Unusual wildlife activity was reported as far away as Redwood, Six Rivers, and Willow Creek, animals fleeing Hoopa and animals running toward it. Two herd of elk clashed at Pyramid Lake, leaving a field on the Nevada border littered with gored carcasses.

The Horrors played the song through to the end—once begun, it must be completed—even though the last of the kitchen staff jumped into the hole five minutes prior. Only Howard, Perky, and Becky were left clapping when they finished. Pegdick stood by the bar, staring at their reflection in the glass behind the bottles. They didn't applaud.

"Gentlemen, I think our work here is done," Howard said, the room silent except for faint screams drifting up from the mine shaft. *Keep on pushing on, show-after-show.*

Santa Monica Pier jutted out into the Pacific Ocean like a dick made of wood, steel, and concrete. The bandshell at the far end hovered fifty feet above the surface of the ocean. *Water, water everywhere*, Vinny thought, *this is going to be bad.*

It was even worse, their most terrifying show yet. People leapt off the pier into the dark, choppy water even before "The Summoning Song" began. Once it did, the killing began in earnest. People killed themselves and each other, were torn apart by sharp-clawed, long-toothed monsters from the sea and sky. Blood slicked the pier's wooden planks. Smart people ran for the exits, only to be stopped by enlightened people who recognized the beginning of the end and embraced the Great Ones' New World Order, a world ruled by madness, murder, and chaos. Screams rose into the Santa Monica night, punctuating "The Summoning Song's" sweeps and swells.

A giant squid washed into the audience, the wet, whipping appendages a fractional part of a much larger creature lurking in the water below the pier. Mouths as wide as man-holes filled with gnashing razor-teeth lined the underside of the thickest tentacles. One whipped toward the stage, and Vinny stepped back. A fishy film sprayed the front of his bass, making the finish bubble and peel.

They can't hurt us as long as we're playing, Vance's

voice echoed in Vinny's head, bringing Vinny zero comfort.

Perky and Becky watched from stage left. One of those horrible toxic arms wrapped around Becky's midsection, lifting her off her feet, pulling her headfirst toward those hungry mouths. Vinny and Perky watched Becky get eaten, three messy bites and gone. Vinny felt bad for Perky, but Perky was expressionless. *Maybe he's glad. It must be a headache having a crew slut for a girlfriend.*

The song ended with four cymbal crashes and the terrible roar of splintered timber. The pier shifted to one side, toppling humans and monsters alike into the water below.

"Fuck!" Vance screamed.

"I think we should go," Thom called out.

"Let's get the fuck out of here!" Vinny shouted. He unstrapped his bass and handed it to Perky. "Weird fucking show tonight."

Perky looked at Vinny with pure hatred.

"You okay, Perk?" Vinny asked. "I'm…I'm sorry about Becky."

Perk shook his head and retreated with Vinny's bass. Another cry of cracked wood filled the night and the pier shifted again. Pegdick struggled getting Thom onto the John Deere, so Vance suggested they use the forklift.

"This whole pier is going into the water," Vance said. "Get his fat ass into the van!"

Vance scooped his keyboards under his arms, while Vinny gathered his foot pedals and cables. Howard ran on stage. Vinny had never seen Howard Phillips run before.

"Let's go, everyone! Show's over! See you in 1974!" *What the hell was Howard talking about?* "Where's Becky?" he asked. Vinny shook his head.

Perky hastily tossed gear into the storage area beneath

the bus. Pegdick rolled up with Thom loaded on the front of the forklift like a dozen plastic garbage bags filled with shit.

"Be careful with my snare!" Thom shouted to Perky. He tried saying more, but Pegdick spilled him into the transit van with a tip of the front forks.

"Peggy and Richard! Please secure the lift," Howard shouted, helping Perky load the bottom of the bus. Howard never helped load equipment. Vinny and Vance joined in. Pegdick locked the forklift to the back of the van and were ready to go by the time Perky, Howard, and the Boyle brothers boarded the bus. As they pulled away from the pier, the boardwalk gave way, splintered planks falling out like old teeth, plunging in the wine-dark sea below.

Vinny retreated to the bedroom. He didn't want to watch Santa Monica pier fall into the Pacific. Vance lay face down on his bunk, sobbing. Vinny sat on the floor next to him and sang "Yesterday" three times, but his brother never joined in.

CHAPTER SIX
Mother

Mom bit Dad's face off in Mexico.

They drove eighteen hours straight after Santa Monica to reach Puebla, parking near the base of a Mayan pyramid, the site of tonight's show. Vinny was sleeping when Thom rang his cell phone.

"Vinny? Get Howard! You gotta come to the van!" Thom said.

"Fuck," Vinny said, images of a pleasant dream—he and Vance surfing—fading. "Call Howard yourself."

"I did. He's not answering," Thom said.

"Call Perky," Vinny grumbled.

"Vinny! You have to get over here! It's…your parents…" Thom didn't finish and Vinny didn't wait for him. He hung up and jumped out of the top bunk.

"Vance!" he said. "Wake up! Something's wrong with Mom and Dad."

"Yes." Vance spoke from the darkness of the bunk, but sounded wide awake. "They're zombies, Vin."

"Not that," Vinny said. "Big Thom called freaking out. Something's wrong with Mom and Dad."

"Let Howard handle it."

"Thom says he's not answering his phone."

"Perky."

"Come on, bro. Let's check it out," Vinny said, but his brother didn't move.

Vinny found Howard and Perky asleep in the front seats of the bus. A thin line of drool ran down Howard's cheek. Disgusting, but at least he was human. Vinny rapped on the window. Perky and Howard awoke startled, but came around quickly.

"Why don't you answer your phone?" Vinny said as Howard and Perky staggered off the bus. "Thom's trying to reach you."

"Because, unlike the rest of you, I am not a slave to electronic devices. I turn my phone *off* when I sleep," Howard said as they approached the transit van. "Now what is…oh dear!"

Richard sat in the driver's seat of the van. His lips were missing, the flesh around his chin torn and ragged. Peggy sat in the passenger seat, the lower half of her face smeared with blood. She chewed as if working a wad of gum.

"Damn it!" Howard pulled open the van door and ordered Peggy out.

"What's going on out there?" Thom Thomas called from the back of the van. No one answered him.

"Peggy, why did you bite Richard's lips off?" Howard asked.

"Hungry," Peggy said.

"Christ, Howard, when's the last time you fed them?" Vinny asked. Richard's eyes rolled toward Vinny. His father's smile was wet, red, and permanent.

"They ate yesterday…but they shouldn't need to eat at all," Howard said. "I don't understand this. This should not have happened."

Howard's confusion scared Vinny. If Howard was lost,

they were all lost, and everything they'd done was mindless chaos and senseless killing. The carefully constructed lie Vinny and Vance lived for the last year came crumbling down without the illusion of Howard's omnipotence.

"Can you…fix this?" Vinny asked.

Howard summoned Richard from the van. Peggy chewed her husband's lips and chin for a good long while before swallowing. Nobody stopped her. Howard examined Richard's mutilated face up close.

"Perky, pliers….shears…something?" Howard said. Perky pulled a wire cutter from his tool belt and handed it to Howard. Howard trimmed away the hanging strings of flesh around Richard's mouth, tossing the scraps on the ground.

"Damn, doesn't that hurt him?" Vinny winced. He wanted to look away but couldn't, his father's soulless blue eyes fixed on him.

Howard plunged the wire cutters several times into Richard's chest. Richard stared straight ahead.

"No, he doesn't feel pain, Vinny!" Howard huffed. "He's not supposed to feel anything. Just do what he's told."

Howard spun and slapped Peggy. Her head smacked against the side of the van. She staggered, but didn't fall.

"And you're not supposed to *eat each other's faces*!" Howard screamed.

"What's going on out there?" Thom called.

"Hey, man! Take it easy!" Vinny said. "She's still my mom."

"Sorry, Vinny, but she messed up," Howard said. "What am I supposed to do with your father now?"

Vinny looked at Richard.

"Get him a surgical mask," Vinny suggested. "Tell

people he's a germaphobe…or a surgeon."

"Grand idea, Vincent. Perhaps if we were touring Asia we could pull it off," Howard said. "But it's hard to walk around with half-a-face in Mexico. People notice. I'm afraid I'll have to deactivate your father. Perky, what else have you got in your belt? A screwdriver?"

"You're going to…kill him?" Vinny asked.

"He's already dead, Vin," Howard said. Vinny shuffled his feet and Howard added, "Your father will finally get the eternal rest he so richly deserves. He was a tremendous asset to our road crew and I'm sure he was a great dad, but it's time to say goodbye."

"Should I…should I get my brother?" Vinny asked.

"Where is he? Why isn't he here?"

"He didn't want to get out of bed," Vinny said.

"Is he taking his medication?"

"Yes," Vinny answered. "But I think this music…this tour…all of it. It's killing him."

"Hey! Can you hear me?" Thom shouted.

Howard frowned. "Well, can you convince your bed-ridden brother to man up and do the job he agreed to do?" he asked. "I haven't even replaced Becky and now I'm down a forklift operator. I'm not even sure how I'm going to get that big bastard out of the van!"

"I can hear you! Rude!" Thom called out. Perky never looked up from his shoes.

"My brother and I never agreed to this," Vinny said.

"You're under contract to perform for Arkham Records," Howard said. "This is all part of the performance."

"Should I get my brother?" Vinny asked again.

"Do you really think he wants to say goodbye to dear old dad, Vin?" Howard hacked into the scar at the base of Richard's skull, twisting Perky's flathead around to widen the opening of the wound.

Vinny couldn't imagine his brother caring about anything anymore. Vance slept a lot. He cried constantly, sad, silent tears.

"No," Vinny said. "I suppose it doesn't matter. Do what you have to do."

Howard rotated the screwdriver handle until the hole in Richard's skull was wide enough to fit Howard's thumb and forefinger. Howard fished around until he found what he was looking for and removed it from Richard's skull with a sharp tug. Vinny couldn't tell if it was a seed, a stone, or a jewel, but as soon as Howard extracted it, Vinny's father collapsed. The light didn't go out of his eyes (*He's already dead, Vin*), but Richard crumpled in a heap and didn't move, even though his blue-eyed gaze never wavered.

"What did you take out of his head?" Vinny asked.

"Nothing to concern yourself about," Howard answered. He flicked fluid off the object and placed it in his shirt pocket, patting the fabric afterward to make sure it was secure. "You could help me out, Vin—help us all out—by talking to your brother and setting his head straight."

Howard turned to Perky.

"You'll take care of Mr. Boyle's remains?" Howard asked. Perky nodded, but never looked up.

"Hey!" Thom called. "I have to take a shit! I need help wiping!"

Howard shuddered and turned toward Peggy.

"I'm very disappointed by your behavior this morning, Mrs. Boyle," Howard said. "I need you to help Mr. Thomas out of the vehicle and with his toileting needs. Please, be careful operating the lift! Because of your actions this morning, Richard is no longer here to help you. You'll to have to get Mr. Thomas off the van by yourself.

Go slowly. Don't tip over."

Peggy turned to go.

"And for God's sake, clean your face!"

Peggy nodded, wiping her bloody mouth with the back of her forearm. Vinny flushed with shame for his mother.

"We're slaves here," Vinny said. "My parents...my brother. You have us all trapped."

"I put you on a rocket ship to success. Your brother too. The two of you have opportunities other musicians can only dream of," Howard said. "Isn't this what you wanted? To be a successful musician?"

"I didn't sign up for black magic bullshit. I didn't sign up for murder, Howard. Neither did Vance. Or our parents," Vinny said. "You suckered all of us. You're using us...to *kill* for you!"

Howard's face grew deep red. He took a breath, held it, let it out. *Smell the pizza, blow out the candles, Howard.* Composure regained, Howard stepped toward Vinny and put a hand on his shoulder. Vinny stepped back, letting Howard's hand fall.

"Listen, Vin. I know you're upset. Last night's show was rough, and now this morning...with your father...it's all very sudden and unfortunate. I apologize if I was curt. This tour is rife with challenges," Howard shark-smiled. "But Vinny, you see what we're doing, right? The majesty of our achievement...the importance of your role. Surely you feel the power and the glory every time you take the stage. The audience appreciates what you're doing. The *universe* appreciates it. "

"No. All I see are monsters and death, Howard," Vinny said. "There's no method to your madness. It's just madness."

"Then you're not looking closely enough, Vincent," Howard said. "Your music is going to change the world. It already has."

"By destroying it?" Vinny said. "By getting everyone eaten alive?"

"By opening the gateway and allowing the world's original owners to reclaim what is rightfully theirs," Howard said.

"I'm not seeing gods, Howard," Vinny said "Only monsters."

"Change your perspective, Vinny! Squint a bit!" Howard said, but his quip fell flat.

"This is killing my brother," Vinny said.

"This gives your brother a sense of purpose!" Howard said. "It gives you both jobs!"

"I told you. This isn't a job. It's slavery," Vinny said. "I quit. Vance, too. Thank you for the opportunity, Mr. Phillips, but we can't continue. My brother has problems with hallucinations and mental breaks, and this environment isn't healthy for him."

Howard looked dumbfounded for a moment before exploding with laughter.

"Vinny, my boy, you *are* funny!" Howard said. "You're under contract with Arkham Records! You're not going anywhere!"

"We'll play tonight," Vinny said. "But that's it. Cancel the rest of the Central American stops."

"Can't do it, Vin," Howard said. "This is business. We have commitments. Life on the road is what separates the men from the boys. Don't be a mannish-boy! Be a man! Be a man for your brother, Vin."

A metallic screech and an earth-shaking crash came from behind the transit van, followed by a string of Thom Thomas epithets.

"Hey! Help! This bitch can't drive for shit!" Thom shouted. Howard locked eyes with Vinny.

"Please, Vincent," Howard said. "We'll get through this. Be strong for your brother. That's all I ask."

"Tonight's show is our last," Vinny said, leaving Howard to deal with Thom Thomas and returning to the tour bus. Vance lay in bed, awake.

"What happened?" he asked.

"Mom ate Dad's face and Howard had to kill Dad. Again," Vinny said. "And I quit the band. You did too. Tonight's show is our last."

"Good. This tour is killing me," Vance said, and Vinny knew it wasn't a figure of speech. "Why did Howie kill Dad if Mom ate his face? Why didn't he kill Mom? Again."

"Because Dad is no longer useful with only half a face," Vinny said. "That's what this is all about, Van. Howard's using us to bring about some kind of musical doomsday."

"I told you that, like, a year ago, but thanks for acknowledging it," Vance said. "You're a good brother."

"Sorry I'm slow, Van," Vinny said. "I tried to keep us out of trouble but I fucked up. Now we're in deep."

"We'll get out," Vance said. "You'll find a way, Vinny. You're good with that stuff."

"I'll try, Van," Vinny said. "In the meantime we have one more show."

"One and done," Vance said. "Let's make it a good one…and not play that evil fucking song."

CHAPTER SEVEN
Jailbreak

The show was brilliant—or terrible, depending on your perspective—and, though Vinny and Vance tried to avoid "The Summoning Song," Thom Thomas demanded it, threatening to sit on Vinny if he didn't agree to play it during the encore.

"There are a lot of people here tonight who came to hear that song," Thom said. "Maybe *you two* don't care about pleasing our fans, but *I* do!"

Vance shrugged and Vinny acquiesced. Thom was in a pissy mood all day. The forklift tipped over earlier, dumping Thom on the ground. He emerged with minor abrasions, but Peggy's arm got pinned under the forklift and broke in two places. A jagged point of bone threatened to tear through the skin near her elbow, though Mom felt no pain. Howard pointed at Mom's useless arm and tossed his hands in the air.

"Another crew hand down!" Howard lamented, dragging Thom's bass drum out of the storage area beneath the bus. "I'm supposed to be the band manager, not a goddamn roadie!"

Perky worked alongside Howard, but he showed no reaction.

Howard dispatched Mom right there on the roadside, digging around in the back of her skull with Perky's screwdriver until a tiny bean popped out of her head and she collapsed.

"Add her to the Offering Chamber, Perky, please," Howard said. Perky dragged Peggy's body around to the far side of the bus. "Peggy was a great woman and she served us well on our musical mission. Your mother will be missed, boys."

"Our mother was a drug addict loser," Vance said.

Vinny felt like grabbing Vance, shaking his ungrateful, mentally-deranged ass until his teeth rattled, shouting in his face, *She loved us the best she could! She self-medicated because of* you! Vinny held his tongue, but wished, not for the first time, he'd been born an only child. Why hadn't he ingested Vance when they were no more than two clumps of cells sharing a womb? Because Vance wouldn't allow it. He demanded his own voice, even though most of the things he said were crazy.

"Parenting is the hardest job in the world...even more difficult than managing a band," Howard smiled, but quickly dropped it when he saw the closed expressions on the brothers' faces. "I'm sure Peggy did the best she could. I don't imagine you boys made it easy on her."

It sounded hollow, but Vinny appreciated Howard's sentiment.

"All she did was mess us up," Vance said. "She leeched off our talent. Both our parents did. They didn't care about us. All they cared about was getting high."

"They had a *disease*, Vance!" Vinny snapped. *Just like you,* he wanted to add.

Perky reappeared from the other side of the bus. He

stuck his head into the cargo area, shifting stuff around, looking for something buried in the back.

"Yeah, a disease called shitparentitis," Vance said. "With a side diagnosis of selfish douchebaggery."

"Evidently *you* inherited *that* from Mom and Dad!" Vinny replied.

Perky pulled a long-handled axe from the cargo hold, removed the protective leather cover, and returned around the side of the bus.

"Stop arguing, boys, and help me move this stuff," Howard said. He handed them each a stack of drums, and, after grabbing an instrument case in each hand, navigated the way toward the stage.

"Despite your personal feelings—and differences—toward your parents, we must accept the fact they are no longer with us," Howard said. "Regardless of how your parents treated you growing up, there's no denying they've been a very valuable asset to this tour and therefore, by proxy, your careers. Your parents helped you when it counted, boys. Try to remember that. And if you figure out how to pull off tonight's show with only me, Perky, and a couple of boneheads working crew, let me know, eh?"

As is often the case, Howard's worry was wasted energy. Three hours before showtime, one hundred members of a cartel called Los Cappas arrived. Speaking through a dark-eyed translator named Juan, the group pledged allegiance to "The Summoning Song," and offered to assist the band in Mexico and Central America. A Los Cappas named Miguel Rodriguez worked the sound board, while other cartel members transported and set up equipment. The rest of Los Cappas worked security.

No amount of security, firepower, or cartel cash prepared them for giant worms emerging from the base of the Mayan Pyramid once "The Summoning Song" began.

Blind, toothy horrors snaked and twisted through the reveling crowd, randomly drawing down victims into a twisting, convulsing terror of slithering, life-crushing appendages.

The band played on. *Last time*, Vinny thought, *We can make it to Mexico City, and fly home tomorrow. Regroup. Restart. Last time…last time…*

Figures appeared atop the pyramid. A team of Los Cappas ran up the stairs to eject the uninvited concert-goers, but the first half-dozen Los Cappas came back down in two pieces, showering the cartel members below with gore, stopping them in their tracks. The creatures atop the pyramid descended, flowed into the audience like black water, an oil spill filled with teeth and claws, cutting down all in its wake. Los Cappas fired guns and ran for the exits with the smart people, while the enlightened danced to the music, bathed in blood, giving themselves wholly to the rough, slouching beast. The worms finished their final sweep as the song came to an end, devouring red scraps before disappearing back down their mysterious, self-sealing holes.

"Great show, guys! The Earthworm Gods are a good sign…a *great* sign! We're getting close," Thom said. "Vance! Where are you going?"

Vinny's brother ran off stage, pausing at the bottom of the stairs to vomit, then spat and stalked toward the bus. Vinny unstrapped his bass and tossed it to a stunned Los Cappas roadie before going after his brother.

"Vance, you okay?" Vinny called.

"No. I'm pretty fucking far from okay." Vance quoted his favorite *Pulp Fiction* line, but it lacked his usual humor.

"It's cool, Vance," Vinny said, catching up with his brother as he boarded the bus. "We're done. Tonight was it. We can pack our shit and go home."

"Actually, boys, I need to talk to you both about that," Howard Phillips said from behind them. Vinny spun around.

"Don't sneak up on us like that, Howard," Vinny said. "It's creepy."

"Sorry, but I needed to talk to you, and assumed I'd find you here," Howard said. "I figured you'd skip the Los Cappas party celebrating the arrival of the Earthworm Gods."

"We're done, Howard," Vinny said. "I told you. My brother and I quit."

"And I told you, that's simply not possible," Howard looked tired and a bit frightened. Vinny liked it. Howard cleared his throat. "You both have signed contracts."

"Those contracts became null and void when you asked us to cut off our toes, asshole," Vance said. "We didn't sign up for self-mutilation."

Howard exhaled slowly.

"That's where you're wrong, Vance," Howard said. "Your toes, along with the other blood sacrifices, made those contracts more binding than ever, binding in a way you can't even imagine. Arkham…the Deacons…I've spoken with them. They're very pleased with the…results you're producing on this tour. I informed them of the various troubles we're having, and they pledged whatever support we need to keep it going. The Los Cappas were likely their doing. They're willing to hire a new, experienced crew when we get back to the states."

"Fuck that," Vinny said.

"They're open to other options as well. A lighter tour schedule…greater compensation…," Howard said. "I must say, rarely have I seen the Deacons so enthusiastic about a group of new artists. I think you guys, all three of you, should talk to the Deacons. Push back a little. I bet they'd be willing…"

"Forget it, Howard," Vance said. "My brother and I leave in the morning. Tour's over."

Vance stepped onto the bus. Vinny went to follow, but Howard grabbed his arm.

"Vincent, please, I need a moment with you," Howard said.

"You heard my brother. We're out of here," Vinny said, but stepped back outside.

"Vinny, I've been instructed to withhold your brother's medication should he refuse to play the contracted shows," Howard said softly. "Arkham will find ways to keep the tour going, easy or hard, Vin."

Vinny lunged but Howard expected the attack and stepped back out of reach. He put his hands up.

"I don't want to," Howard said from several paces away. "But I will if I have to. Don't make me, Vinny."

Howard disappeared into the night, presumably to join the big Earthworm Gods party. Vinny considered chasing Howard down and beating him up, but it wouldn't solve anything. Howard followed orders. His job sucked too.

Vinny put his head in his hands, his lower back tense, the world resting on his shoulders. He was supposed to watch over Vance, keep his brother safe, and instead he'd led him into an inescapable trap. Vinny spat in the dirt and boarded the bus. Vance lay on his bunk, hidden in darkness.

"I think we have to play another show," Vinny spoke into the dark. "The day after tomorrow, in Belize. Then we go back to the states. It'll be easier for us to split once we're back home." *And easier to get your meds…even a walk-in clinic or hospital could help*, Vinny thought.

Vance was quiet for so long, Vinny thought his brother

had fallen asleep.

"I knew we couldn't get out…" the whispered voice that emerged from the dark bunk was so broken and weak, it could have been their mother's.

Belize City was another terrible success. The monsterpus that tore apart Santa Monica pier showed up again, washing ashore with a mouth as wide as a soccer field, devouring half the audience in one gulp, lashing the survivors with an endless stream of toothy tentacles. It ate through the crowd, sat chewing bodies, placidly watching the band wrap up "The Summoning Song," before letting the waves carry it back out to sea. *How did it get here from Santa Monica? Did it pass through the Panama Canal? Swim around the tip of South America? Was it the same creature or one that looked like it? How could there be* two *of those things?* But Vinny knew nothing existed in a vacuum—there is always more than one.

Perky stood stage left, a gun in his hand, watching the monster that ate his girlfriend recede back into the ocean.

"Shoot the fucking thing, Perk!" Vinny shouted, but maybe Perky couldn't hear him over the music.

They packed up quickly after the show. The Belize chapter of Los Cappas was rowdier than its Mexican counterpart, and wanted to party with the band. Only Thom Thomas joined them. Somehow the Los Cappas got Thom aloft and passed his immense body over the top of the crowd. Vinny was impressed with their commitment and courage.

Vinny and Vance retreated to the bus. Their duffel bags were packed and five minutes later their Uber arrived to take them to the airport. They were booked on a flight to Panama City, Florida, where the band was scheduled to play a state fair the following night. *Technically later today*, Vinny thought, checking the time on his phone.

They'd arrive three hours before the rest of the crew, and a 24-hour clinic/pharmacy in Panama City could refill Vance's risperidone and Seroquel. Injectable fluphenazine would be harder to come by, but they could hit a hospital once they caught a flight home. The timing worked out perfectly; they'd be gone from Panama City before the crew even arrived from Belize.

"We did it, Vance! We survived the Endless Tour," Vinny said. He meant it as a joke, but looking at Vance, his brother's head back against the window, eyes closed, tissue jammed up his nose to stifle yet another nose-bleed, it didn't feel funny. It seemed a statement of fact, something a wounded soldier might say upon returning from a harrowing tour of duty. Vance looked like he'd been through a war, a war fought from the inside out. "We're veterans of the psychic wars, bro!"

Vance managed a wan smile.

"I'm burnin' for you, Vinny," he croaked. "Don't fear the reaper."

"That's the spirit," Vinny said. "Bummer we had to leave our gear behind, but we'll get new stuff back home. Maybe join a wedding band or something."

"Color my world with *hope*, Vin," Vance said. Even in jest, Vinny liked hearing his brother say the word aloud.

They caught their flight and slept on the plane. Vinny's dreams were filled with deep-sea nightmares, but every time he awoke, Vance slept peacefully, which made him feel better. They were going to make it, get back home, and hit the reset button on their lives. *Maybe I can go back to Chancellor and see if they have teaching jobs for Vance and me,* Vinny thought. If not…wedding bands were easy money. Everybody do the Electric Slide, boogie-oogie-oogie!

The plane landed in Panama City just after dawn, sunrise

spilling into the cabin on pink shafts of light. They had lousy seats near the back of the plane. Vinny put a hand on his brother's shoulder as they waited to disembark.

"We're gonna be okay, bro," Vinny said, and his brother smiled back at him. They would have been too…if Howard Phillips wasn't waiting for them at the gate.

CHAPTER EIGHT

Tom's Diner

How was it possible? How could Howard arrive in Panama City ahead of them? Vinny supposed anything was possible with helicopters, private jets, and ample funding, but alarm bells went off in his head. Had Howard tapped his phone? Was their bedroom bugged? Could Howard read their minds?

Two tall African-American men stood behind Howard. The men resembled each other—one younger, one older—and Vinny thought they might be security guards, except the older man was too old and too well-dressed to be muscle.

"Good morning, Vincent. Good morning, Vance. I hope you had an enjoyable flight," Howard sounded chipper, but his eyes were sad. "I'd like you to meet the Deacons, William Jr. and William Sr., the president and vice president of Arkham Records and Recording."

"You gotta be shitting me," Vance said. He looked ready to cry.

The younger man stepped forward and offered his hand to Vance.

"Good to finally meet you in person, Vance," he said. "I'm William Deacon Jr. I'd like to thank you for all the hard work you and your brother have put into this tour. My grandfather and I are big fans."

"Thank you," Vance muttered, shaking William Jr.'s hand. He glanced at Vinny, looking like an animal trapped in a cage. William Jr. shook Vinny's hand next.

"Appreciate you catching the earlier flight today, Vin," William Jr. said. His eyes twinkled, his palm ice cold. "I always got to the next gig as soon as possible back when I toured. More time to settle in and warm up, the better the show, right?"

Vinny nodded stupidly, at a loss for words. *How could this be happening?*

"The Deacons want to buy you breakfast," Howard said. "I'm sure you boys worked up an appetite on your early morning travels."

Food was the last thing on Vinny's mind, but he and his brother followed Howard and the Deacons through the airport terminal to a nondescript door near the food court. Howard showed a badge to a security guard who opened the door. They ascended a staircase (William Sr. quite slowly) where Howard showed his badge again. They entered a private dining room overlooking the tarmac, the decor aged leather, dark wood, and desolation. The five of them were alone in the vast room until a server appeared and showed them to a table near the windows. The view was beautiful and when the server returned with five glasses of orange juice, William Jr. ordered breakfast for the entire table: bacon, eggs, pancakes, potatoes. Every item he mentioned made Vinny's stomach flip.

William Jr. raised a glass of orange juice after the server left and everyone followed suit. Vance's hand shook, and Vinny couldn't stop watching his juice slosh around, threatening to spill over the rim of the glass.

"Cheers, gentlemen!" William Jr. said. "Here's to the

most talented new band on the Arkham Records roster!"

"Here, here!" Howard said.

"Thom's not here. He's part of the band too," Vance said, his voice steadier than his hands.

"Indeed, he is. An important part," William Jr. said, holding his orange juice over the table until they all clinked glasses. Nobody drank except for William Sr., and Vinny saw a few drops of juice fall from the old man's mouth and land on his tie. "That boy's kick drum is a force of nature. But you know Thom's size makes it hard for him to attend certain functions."

"He never could have made it up those stairs," Howard said. He leveled a cold eye at Vinny. "Plus, you boys opted for an early flight. Thom is still traveling from Belize."

"My grandfather and I wanted to talk with the two of you privately, anyhow," William Jr. said. The server came again and poured coffee. Vinny fought the urge to drink it. He didn't want to break bread with their captors. But the fresh roast smelled so good, he took a sip...and another. Excellent coffee.

"We know this is a very difficult tour for you and your family. First, let me start by saying my grandfather and I are truly sorry for what happened to your parents," William Jr. said. *What part?* Vinny wondered. *Their deaths? Their rebirth? Their dismemberment?* "We promise to get you adequate crew support for your upcoming shows in the states. And ample time off. After tonight, you've got the next six days free and we're keeping the schedule to no more than two or three shows per week."

"This will work out better for Thom, as well," Howard said. "The physical demands of a heavy tour schedule are quite challenging for him."

Vinny shook his head and opened his mouth, but his brother surprised him by speaking first.

"We're quitting the band," Vance said. "No more shows. Tonight or ever."

The server and a busboy picked that moment to arrive and load the table with steaming plates of food. No one spoke until they left.

"Vinny and Vance are under the impression their contracts are negotiable," Howard said, never looking up from his bacon and eggs. "I did my best to convince them otherwise."

"We're not playing that song anymore," Vance said. "I…I can't…"

"Sure you can!" William Jr. said. "You're an amazing musician and you do that song justice! We appreciate how you gentlemen bring the song to life. Hell, the *song* appreciates it! Can't you feel it? Don't you feel how the whole world resonates as one whenever you play it?"

"All I see is death," Vance said. "It makes me feel terrible. Sick to my stomach."

"What is that song?" Vinny asked. "What is it doing? Where does it come from?"

"There are no simple answers to your questions, Vin, but I'll do my best." William Jr. said. "The song is property of Arkham Records and Recording. It's been in our archives for many, many years. The song is credited to my great-grandparents, Sonny Deacon and Wilma Walters, but there's evidence suggesting the song's origins are much older. As for what the song does…let me ask, what do *you* see when you play that song, Vinny?"

Vinny didn't care for William Jr.'s armchair psychologist tone.

"You're not going to pretend the monsters aren't real, are you?" Vinny asked. "Those things have been devouring our fans since we hit the road. What *are* they?"

"That music…that song…can induce a trance-like,

hypnotic state," William Jr. said. "You can't always believe what you see during that song…it'll fool you."

"We're being fooled, all right, but not by 'The Summoning Song,'" Vance said. "It's clear what that song is. It's pure evil. A gateway to hell."

"You make it sound so dramatic, Vance," William Jr. smiled. "But it's an optical illusion. The song opens a doorway, but not to a dimension of man-eating monsters. It opens a doorway in the deepest recesses of the human mind."

"Bullshit. Bullshit." Vance coughed into his fist.

"How do you keep the media away? The police?" Vinny asked. "People are dying! People are missing!"

"People aren't missing if they go willingly," Howard said, but William Jr. stopped him with a raised palm.

"Know why the police aren't investigating mass murder at your shows, Vinny? Because *you're* the only one seeing it," William Jr. said, and Vinny hated how logical it sounded, how much sense it made. "The song compels people to see what they want to see, believe what they want to believe. If you guys see death and monsters…well, it's understandable given all you've been through. Arkham Records has excellent mental healthcare professionals available under your current insurance plan."

What if Vance's mental delusions had *leaked* over to Vinny? Weird stuff happens between twins. If his twin brother was schizophrenic, how far away from mental illness could Vinny be?

"Get someone else to play your song," Vance said. "Why us?"

William Jr. looked at his grandfather and Howard before speaking.

"We have other artists under contract with Arkham, of course," William Jr. said. "But none we have more confidence in than you. You're the best musicians we have and you connect with the piece on a very natural, almost primal, level. We believe in you."

Something swelled in Vinny's chest. It might have been pride coming from Peg or Rich, but from William Jr. it was only heartburn.

"What's your end-game?" Vinny asked.

"Global unity through art and music," William Jr. said. "A new world order. You have our word, there will be a place of honor for the Boyle brothers in the new administration."

Howard gave them both a slight nod.

"What's up with all the Lovecraft shit?" Vance asked. "The Dunwich Horrors? Arkham Records? Shit's cheesy, AF. Can't we be a normal band?"

Howard Phillips shot icy daggers at the Boyles, but William Jr. laughed.

"It *is* a little over the top, right?" he chuckled. "And our headquarters are in Providence, no less! But there's a link between fantastical literature and music that runs deep and Lovecraft's work coincides with many of our company's projects."

"Did Lovecraft write 'The Summoning Song'?" Vinny asked.

"No," William Jr. shook his head. "Lovecraft couldn't conceive of something so great. Plus, the origins of the song pre-date Lovecraft by a good many years."

"Did Erich Zann write it?" Vance asked. William Jr. waved a dismissive hand.

"Erich Zann is a fictional character Lovecraft created," William Jr. said. "Nothing more. Don't read too much into it, fellas."

Vinny clenched his jaw and stared into William Jr.'s eyes.

"Is Howard Phillips, our manager, actually H.P. Lovecraft, the writer?"

William Jr. and Sr. burst out laughing. Vinny feared the old man might lose his teeth. Howard Phillips smiled at the Boyles.

"Go ahead, Vinny," Howard said, turning his head and showing Vinny the back of his neck. "I know you're dying to check."

Despite himself, Vinny checked. No "X" at the base of Howard's skull. He hated how the Deacons laughed, like a witch's cackle.

"Oh, that's funny, Vin! You thought *your* H.P. was *the* H.P.!" William Jr. said. "This is why we love working with artists like you and your brother. You're amazingly creative thinkers."

"How did you bring our parents back?" Vinny asked, pleased when their laugher faded. "They were dead. Cold. Then Howard put a magic bean in their heads and they came back to life…only different. Did we imagine that too?"

"See? Magic bean.That's the kind of creative thinking I'm talking about," William Jr. said, but his tone was serious and he never broke eye contact with Vinny. "Arkham has acquired certain metaphysical assets which we employ, on rare occasions, to help facilitate various business ventures. If there's a need, Arkham will find a way. We thought it would be a comfort to you and your brother—as well as a help to us on the road crew—to have your parents along on your first tour. We hope we didn't overstep our bounds. We realize your parents suffered some unforeseen trauma on the tour and we're sorry you had to witness that. Hindsight's always twenty/twenty and the road to hell is paved with good intentions, Vinny. We're sorry if we made mistakes with your parents."

"If you ask me, you're better off," Howard said between mouthfuls of bacon. He was the only one eating, shoveling food in like it was his last meal. "Peggy and Richard were far better parents dead than alive. The drugs? The drama? The revolving door of addictions? Terrible."

"Nobody asked you!" Vinny said. "And you're the one who sold my mother the drugs that killed her!"

The Deacons scowled at Howard, and Howard nearly choked on his eggs.

"What are you talking about?"

"My mother bought drugs at your studio," Vinny said. "That's why she took my brother there for oboe lessons. You sold her the drugs that killed her."

"I assure you, I did not," Howard Phillips said. "I pride myself on keeping my studio drug-free and would never allow drug dealing in or around my place of business. I can't be responsible for whom your mother met with—students or non-students—outside of the studio environment. Drug addicts are like rats, they sniff out dealers, find them in any and every environment. I suspect this was the case with your mother. But it had nothing to do with me or my studio. Drug addicts eventually overdose and die. I'm sorry that happened to your parents, Vincent, but please don't blame me for their lifetime of mistakes and bad choices."

Howard returned to his eggs. Vinny hoped his brother would back him up, come to his parents' defense.

"Resurrecting the dead is a rather major metaphysical asset, as you call it," Vance said. "Where did Arkham acquire this ability? And why not stick magic beans in Jimi Hendrix and Keith Moon, get them to play your dumb song?"

"I like the way you think, Vance," William Jr. said, giving a thumbs up. "We have partners all over the world and in worlds beyond that supply us with the resources we need. We have a boss, too, Vance, and if you think we're assholes, you should meet her!"

William Jr. laughed, and William Sr. raised his bushy eyebrows.

"Plus, as Vinny pointed out, people come back different. Some have dexterity and coordination issues. They often lack the…the *spirit* they once had, the spirit artists need to create. They go through the motions, but it doesn't have the same *feel*."

"One of your imaginary monsters wrapped a tentacle around me at last night's show," Vance said. "And another ate our roadie's girlfriend. We're not making this stuff up. Listen to how stupid it sounds!"

"What you're seeing and perceiving as real *does* sound crazy," William Jr. said. "That's the beauty of this song, the power of it, the way it alters the human mind. It changes perception and puts people in a different mind-set. Imagine if all the world heard this song…imagine all the people, living in a world of peace! Global peace at last, everyone moving and dancing as one, *listening* as one! The song needs *you* to reach its full potential, gentlemen."

"It's killing us," Vinny said. "Especially my brother."

"What doesn't kill you makes you stronger, as Ms. Clarkson says," William Jr. said. "I assure you, no harm will come your way as long as you're playing the song."

"With all due respect, Mr. Deacon, I don't believe you," Vinny said. "This song is about chaos and destruction, not peace."

"You've got to break a few eggs to make an omelet, Vin," William Jr. said.

"What's the omelet? The end of the world?" Vinny asked. "Our world is a troubled, fucked-up place, but my brother and I want to keep living in it, so, no thank you."

"It's not a choice you have, Vin," William Jr. said.

"Are you threatening us?" Vinny said.

"You leave and you die," William Sr. spoke for the first time, his voice so deep, it made Vinny's scrotum tingle. "That's not a threat. It's a fact. The song won't let you leave. You made the blood offering. You're in now."

"The three of you are going to physically stop us from walking out of here and catching a flight home?" Vance asked. He shifted in his seat, coiled tension radiating off him. *Smell the pizza, blow out the candles, Vance.*

"Don't be silly, Vance! You'd kick our asses…though I don't know why you'd want to beat up my poor ol' grandpa," William Jr. said. "Finish your breakfast and leave. We're cool. But the song will bring you back eventually. It always does. What does Blues Traveler say? 'It's the hook that brings you back'. It's like that."

"Song killed my son, Billy, when he tried to quit," William Sr. said, an uncomfortable silence falling over the table. "Kill you too if you try to run."

CHAPTER NINE

Panama

"You ready for this, bro?" Vinny asked.

Vance didn't look ready for anything, his eyes glassy and unfocused. He slumped on the piano bench, ready to fall over if not for his white-knuckled grip on the edge of the baby grand.

"Cool, bro," Vance said, drawing the syllables out. *What the hell was he on?* Vinny gave his brother an extra Seroquel tablet this morning and they'd smoked a joint twenty minutes ago, but this was something else. Had Howard slipped Vance something to keep him going through the show? He'd become comfortably numb.

They'd upgraded up from a bus to a trailer. Howard and Perky stopped by earlier because Vance locked himself in his bedroom.

"Damn it, Vance! Open the door!" Howard pounded on it hard, but Vance wouldn't answer. "Come on, Vance! I thought we straightened everything out at breakfast this morning?"

Howard spoke quietly to Vinny.

"How long has he been in there?"

"A couple of hours."

"Christ on a stick! It's like dealing with a teenage girl!"

Howard said. "Perky, get the axe. We'll have to pull him out of there.

"The axe is back on the bus in Belize, Mr. Phillips," Perky said.

"Fuck me twice! Get some tools to remove this door!"

"Don't," Vinny said. "I'll get him out. We'll play tonight. Just leave us alone."

"I appreciate the way you look out for your brother, Vincent," Howard said. "But this might be beyond your abilities. Let us help."

"If you want to help, don't break down my brother's door," Vinny said. "He needs...time...to prepare for tonight's show. We've got three hours. Just leave us be."

"If I don't hear from you, I'll be back in an hour to check on your progress," Howard said. He and Perky left.

Vinny lit a cigarette and sat cross-legged in front of Vance's door. He flicked ashes on the floor.

"Howard and Perky dropped by to say hello," he said. "You may have heard Howard's gentle rapping upon your door."

"Howard's an asshole," came Vance's muffled reply. "And Perky's lost without Becky."

This surprised Vinny. He hadn't noticed any change in Perky's behavior, but his brother was always more observant.

"Howard will be back in an hour," Vinny said. "He's worried you're going to bail on tonight's gig."

"You lied to me, Vinny," Vance said after a long pause. "You promised last night was the last time."

"I know I did, Van," Vinny flicked his butt into the bathroom next to Vance's bedroom. It bounced off the toilet lid and landed in the water with a hiss. "I'm sorry, bro. I truly am. I tried to get us out. We'll find another way."

"There is no other way, Vinny," Vance said. "We're trapped inside Arkham. It won't let us out."

"Let's take it one show at a time, Vance," Vinny said. "We get through tonight and we have a week off."

"I don't think I can play it again tonight," Vance muttered from the other side of the door. "I really don't think I can."

"You can do it, Vance. *We* can do it. I'll be with you," Vinny said. "Smell the pizza and blow out the candles. Just breathe. We'll get through this."

Vance didn't agree to play, but he emerged from the bedroom. The two of them strummed guitars, smoked pot, and ate Twinkies until it was time for the show. Vance didn't drink or take any more drugs—Vinny was with him nearly all day—but Vance was a mess now, unsteady and incoherent.

"What's wrong with your brother?" Thom called from behind the drum kit.

"He's fine," Vinny called back.

"Doesn't look fine," Thom said. "Is he gonna be able to play? Big crowd tonight."

"He can play," Vinny said to Thom. "Just keep the beat going and we'll handle the rest."

They opened with a cover of "Yesterday," which helped bring Vance around. They flowed into "Collie Flower Stew." Vinny stretched each section, Vance filling the gaps with blazing keyboard fills. "Stew" gave way to "Lucille," and Vinny never heard his brother play more beautifully, every note filled with longing, every phrase a cry from the deepest depths of his tortured soul. Through music, Vance finally cried for the loss of their parents, their youth, their innocence. Vance mourned the loss of his sanity in every note he played, sad melodies dripping from his fingertips. Vinny cried too.

By the time "The Summoning Song" rolled around, the Gulf of Mexico teemed with sea-life—fins, tails, and teeth making the surface of the water churn. An inky shadow the size of an oil rig rose from the sea, cast ten-thousand unblinking yellow eyes towards the shore and slowly submerged again. A thick, impenetrable cloud rained living creatures—part frog, part crab, part lobster, with toothsome mouths half the length of their bodies—that bit and tore through the audience, scurrying underfoot, sinking fangs into tender Achilles tendons, the solid meat of heels, a buffet of severed toes. The worms returned, but smaller than in Belize. Humanoid creatures crawled from the gulf and staggered into the crowd, dancing with the dead and feasting on the living. One walked to the front of the stage, its face nothing but a black hole with teeth. Vinny thought monsterpus wallowed in the shallows, a super-sized, super-fan following the band all the way from Belize, but the creature never came closer than the beach.

Don't be shy monsterpus! Come up for a bite to eat! Your arms must be starving! Vinny giggled. Vance smiled too, his hands drifting to-and-fro over the keyboards. Vinny's brother was happiest—and most normal—playing music. Vance looked alive when "The Summoning Song" filtered through him, a living conduit for its dark beauty.

Thom's glistening bulk jiggled in time to the beat; his kick drum really *was* a force of nature. A blister burst on Vinny's finger, leaving a tiny blotch of blood and water around the fifth fret. He ground the wound against the steel strings, feeling nothing, and played on.

Perky stood next to the stage, the gun in his hand. *Protecting the band*, Vinny thought. *Hey Perk, didn't you get the memo? They can't hurt us as long as we're playing!* Vinny's laughter went on and on and he wondered if he'd finally lost his mind.

The song closed with four hard cymbal crashes, but Perky ran on stage before the final crash and blew his brains out. There was a strange moment—a moment of odd *relief*—when Vinny was sure Perky would shoot him and his brother…probably Thom too. *Do it, Perk. We've got it coming.* But Perky faced the audience, put the gun under his chin, and fired a round through his brain. The bullet exited the top of Perky's skull, blowing his Shure Microphones cap off, speckling Vinny with blood.

"Oh shit!" Thomas yelled. "What the fuck, Perky?"

Vinny didn't understand why Thom yelled at Perky's corpse, but nobody was thinking clearly. Vance stood and came around the front of his keyboards, staring down at Perky's body, head cocked to one side like a dog hearing a funny sound. Vinny held his arms out, shaking. *It's blood. It's Perky's blood. I feel it dripping down my face.*

Two Los Cappas roadies drew the stage curtains. Howard Phillips rushed in from the wings and knelt beside Perky.

"Damn it, Perky!" Howard said. "What did you do?"

Why do they yell at the dead man? Howard moved Perky's head from side-to-side. Brains sloshed out the exit wound.

"*Argh!* I can't do anything with this!" Howard sounded disgusted. He waved two Los Cappas over, and spoke to them in fluent Spanish. *I didn't know Howard spoke a second language,* Vinny thought dully. He wiped his face, and his hands came away red. *Perky's blood.*

Vance's head remained cocked to one side, his smile serene as he watched the Los Cappas grab Perky's boots and drag him away. Perky's ruined head left a red streak like spilled paint across the stage.

"Shit! That's fucked up!" Thom called out from the drum riser. "Somebody get me down from here!"

"Thom! Can't you see I'm dealing with an emergency situation?" Howard snapped. "Sit tight and someone will come by shortly with the forklift to fetch you."

"I can't see anything! Get me down so I can see what's happening!" Thom whined.

Becky and Perky are together again, playing harps on a cloud with Pegdick. Vinny smiled and looked over at his brother, eager to share the joke. But his brother stared down at Perky's gun.

"Vance!" Vinny shouted. Vance didn't respond until Vinny shouted his name a second time. "Be cool, man. Let's get back to the trailer and chill out, figure out our next step."

Vance smiled, sad and bashful.

"I figured it out, Vin," Vance said.

"No!"

Suddenly the bass around Vinny's neck felt heavy and cumbersome. He lifted the instrument over his head and invisible hands (*Los Cappas'?*) grabbed the instrument away from him, but it was already too late. Vance had Perky's gun.

"Don't do it, Vance!" Vinny screamed. "We'll figure a way out!"

"What the hell is going on?" Howard said, aware of a sudden temperature change on stage. He stood beside Vinny.

"What's happening?" Thom yelled from the drum riser.

"There is no other way, Vin. The song's inside us now," Vance said, voice calm, almost too quiet to hear. "There's only Perky's way. He knew."

"Vance!" Howard shouted. "Please don't do this!"

Vance lifted the gun and for a glorious, heart-stopping moment Vinny thought he might turn the weapon on Howard. *Do it! Put one right between his eyes, Vance!*

Save us all!

But his brother only saved himself. He put the barrel of the gun to his temple and pulled the trigger. The roar of the shot filled Vinny's head until it was all he heard.

"Hey! What's going on?" Thom called. "What happened? Hey? Hey!"

CHAPTER TEN

Interlude: Little Willy

1 — *Lincoln Center, New York City. February 4, 1977.*

Avery Fisher Hall had integrity and class back when it was called the Philharmonic. Some fat cat makes a donation and they rename the whole damn building after him? Screw Avery Fisher! Half-assed fiddle playin' asshole, plastering his name all over everything. It reeked of corporate bullshit, as far as Smoke Johnson was concerned.

Still, the box at Avery Fisher—replete and regal with studded, brown leather chairs and crushed velvet bunting—was pretty damn nice. Smoke looked forward to an evening with Dave Brubeck and Paul Desmond. Everybody knew Des was dying and there weren't many gigs left.

Smoke's peace ended when William Deacon II entered the box alongside a weasel-like man Smoke didn't recognize. Smoke jumped up, but William and the stranger blocked the exit. Smoke looked over the edge of the box. Could he survive a jump into the orchestra seats?

"Relax, Smoke," William said. "My father sent me to kill you, but I don't want to. Let's sit down."

"How did you get in here?" Smoke asked.

William spread his hands.

"This is Arkham's box," he said. "You're here at our invitation."

"Brubeck himself invited me," Smoke said.

"Of course," William said. "We knew you wouldn't come otherwise."

Smoke glowered at William Deacon.

"Sneaky bastards, you Arkham folk," Smoke said. "Persistent, too."

"Takes a sneak to catch a sneak, Smoke," William said. "I'd like you to meet David, a big fan of your music."

Weasel-man grabbed Smoke's hand and shook vigorously.

"It's an honor to meet you, Mr. Johnson! A true honor!" David gushed, eyes moist, near tears. "I've followed you…for months. Your music is an inspiration."

"You a fan of the blues?" Smoke wanted to extract his hand from David's clammy grip.

"Not really," David said. He finally let go of Smoke's hand, but wouldn't stop staring and smiling. "I-I can't believe it's really you."

"Take a seat over there, David, and enjoy the show." William broke up the awkward moment and pointed David toward a chair. "I need to speak with Smoke privately."

David sat and Smoke and William took the two chairs furthest from him.

"You know who David is?" William asked.

Smoke shook his head.

"He knows you," William said. "Been to all your performances since you got here last summer."

"Never saw him before," Smoke said. "I got fans all over."

"Do you remember a show in Pelham Bay the end of last

July?" William asked.

"No," Smoke shook his head. "Why should I?"

"How about your October 23 performance at the Romper Room in Flushing? You remember that one?" William asked. "Or the Grindhouse on November 27?"

Brubeck opened with "Take Five." The audience burst into applause, but Smoke wasn't listening.

"Lotta gigs, you know?" Smoke said. "Can't remember them all."

"Surely you remember playing at the Track Shack in Flushing last week," William said. "You played a certain song at all those shows, Smoke. A song that's property of Arkham Records…a song belongs to my grandfather, Sonny Deacon."

Smoke crumpled before William's eyes, aged twenty years in a matter of seconds. He put his face in his hands and sobbed loud enough to make a few people seated in the orchestra look up. David, oblivious, stared at the stage with child-like wonder. Paul Desmond was blowing hard tonight, lung cancer be damned.

"Listen to your father, William. Kill me." Smoke wiped his eyes, slumped in his chair. "Put me out of my misery. I'm tired of running from Arkham, tired of trying to dump that damned song! It's an albatross, and I can't shed it, man. Can't quit it neither. Kill me. Make your Daddy happy."

"Call me Billy," William said.

"I'll call you Deke," Smoke said. "That's what I called your grandfather."

"Did you really kill my grandfather?"

Smoke rubbed his face.

"I was a kid," he said. "Your grandfather murdered your grandmother. Did you know that? Your grandmother was about the sweetest person on earth and your grandfather was a monster. That song *made* him a monster."

"Some songs demand sacrifice," William said.

"Endless sacrifice. It's never enough," Smoke said. "That song makes people do terrible things."

William nodded toward David, who sat enraptured by Brubeck and Desmond blasting through "Blue Turk."

"David's got a .44-caliber handgun under his jacket," William said. "He's a shit shot, but he's…determined. Your music moves him, Smoke. The blood sacrifice gets made, even if someone else does it for you."

Smoke rubbed his face again. He recognized David now, from police sketches in the newspapers.

"You brought him here to shoot me?" Smoke asked.

William shook his head.

"We'd have to get you a date to finger-bang down on Lover's Lane first," William chuckled. "There are worse ways to go, I suppose."

"Look, just do it, man!" Smoke jumped out of his seat again. "Fucking *kill me now*!"

Faces turned toward the commotion in Smoke's box.

"Thank you very much!" Brubeck called out before introducing his backing band.

"Sit down, Smoke," William said gently. "Don't cause a scene."

Smoke spun on David, hoping to surprise the young man into firing. But David studied Smoke placidly, the nowhere smile never leaving his face. Smoke sat down.

"My father wants to kill you, Smoke, but I don't," William said. "I've heard the stories about my grandparents and I'm inclined to believe you. My grandfather was a notorious asshole. And my grandma was a special lady. All the musical talent comes from her side of the family.

"I got a son of my own now, Smoke, and I don't want

any more blood on my family's hands," William said. "This has to stop."

"Song's been around forever, Deke," Smoke said. "How you gonna stop it?"

"It's not a bad song, Smoke. But it needs proper guidance," William said. "Not all the doors it opens lead to bad places. Some are glorious."

"None I've seen," Smoke said.

"Have you ever inverted it?" William asked. "Flipped the song around, played it back to front, so each note is mirrored with its harmonic opposite?"

"No," Smoke said.

"If you try it, you may find the song is vastly different from what you're accustomed to," William said. "For all your improvisational skills, Smoke, I'm surprised you hadn't tried it before."

Smoke's cheeks flushed.

"This sounds like more Arkham bullshit," Smoke said. "Your old man been chasin' me for years. Now you got me. Your button man's sitting right there. Be done with this. Please. I'm ready."

"*I'm* not ready, Smoke," William said. "I told you, I have no interest in avenging my grandfather. I need to end this, stitch up the Infinitus once and for all…and I'll need your help."

"How?"

"David is going to invite you to a party and introduce you to some of his friends," William said. "Accept the invitation. Go to the party."

"Why the hell would I want to party with the .44 Caliber Killer?" Smoke asked.

"David's friends are powerful," William said. "Have you heard of The Process Church?"

"Ain't that devil shit?" Smoke asked. "Ain't we in

enough trouble without bringing Satan into this mess?"

William smiled.

"You're a fool if you think he's not involved already, but this isn't about what The Process Church believes," William said. "It's about siphoning *the power* of that belief to seal the Infinitus. Faith is a powerful tool, Smoke. I'm sure you've borrowed tools before. Bet you forgot to return a few, too, huh?"

"You sound crazy," Smoke said.

"I'm not the one begging to die. *That's* crazy," William said. "What I'm suggesting is no crazier than the shit you've seen—and done—so far."

Smoke sighed.

"What do I have to do?"

2 — *Columbia University, New York City. March 8, 1977.*

"Smoke Johnson, it's my pleasure to introduce you to Mary Ann and Robert de Grimston, founders of The Process Church of the Final Judgement."

David delivered each word with care and precision. Smoke got the impression he'd rehearsed this introduction several times, probably in front of a mirror. William gave David a "good job" nod and Smoke shook hands with Mary Ann and Robert.

"Pleased to meet you," Smoke said. "You must be the freaky-deaky devil worshippers David has told me so much about!"

David turned a whiter shade of pale, but Mary Ann laughed, loud and joyous, and Robert smiled.

"Don't tease David like that, Mr. Johnson!" Robert chided. "You'll give him a heart attack…and then where would we be?"

Mary Ann laughed again, positively howled, and Smoke couldn't help but smile along with her. He liked her vibe.

"We worship Jesus Christ, too, Mr. Johnson," Mary Ann said, wiping away a tear. "Someday Christ and Satan will be joined as one for the Final Judgement."

"Of course," Smoke replied. "I like to hear more about it, but I have another set to play."

"I hope you'll play the special song David has told us so much about," Mary Ann winked at Smoke. "Your music is such an influence on him."

"It would be an honor," Smoke said. "And, as a special treat, I'm gonna have my friend Deke join me on keys."

"Deke!" Robert said, his eyes and smile wide. "I like that name, Billy! It suits you."

"Don't tell my father," William said, and Mary Ann laughed again.

"I've know you since you were a little boy, Billy, and never once, in all the years your father and I worked together, have I heard you play piano," Mary Ann said. "Tonight is really going to be a treat!"

Smoke made the de Grimstons happy and played the song they came to hear, William matching him note-for-note two octaves up the scale. They played until the air inside Columbia University Performing Arts Center shimmered and faceless shadows with too many limbs, eyes, and teeth crawled, circled, and stalked the auditorium. Mary Ann looked positively orgasmic. Smoke gave William the nod. Time to wrap. Enough for tonight.

The de Grimstons cornered William and Smoke backstage, lavishing praise upon them. David slipped out the back entrance, waited until 19-year-old Virginia Voskerichian walked by, and drew his gun. Virginia raised her stack of textbooks to defend herself, but David's bullet penetrated the books and struck Virginia in the head, killing her. He stepped back into the auditorium.

"Can I give anyone a lift home?" he asked.

The de Grimstons declined and said their goodbyes, promising to attend William and Smoke's next performance. Smoke and William accepted David's offer, but Smoke changed his mind once he saw David's yellow Volkswagen by the curb.

"You driving a Ted Bundy mobile, David?" Smoke asked.

"I don't know him," David answered. "Is he in The Process?"

Smoke and William hailed a cab.

They played the following month at a place called Big Beaters in the Bronx. Mary Ann and Robert came, along with David. While the de Grimstons treated Smoke and William to a post-show cocktail, David walked along Pelham Bay until he found a steamed-up car. He fired several times through the passenger window, killing twenty-year-old Alexander Essau, and eighteen-year-old Valentina Suriani. He arrived back at Big Beaters in time to offer the de Grimstons a ride home. They accepted.

"What the fuck we doing, man?" Smoke asked after David and the de Grimstons left. "How many times we gonna perform like damn monkeys for these crazy fucks? We're getting David all riled up."

"We play until they invite us to perform at one of their group rituals," William said. "I figured they would have by now."

They finally did after Smoke and William's next show. BayLaid in Bayside, Queens filled with spirits and shadows and David couldn't contain himself. In release and celebration he fired three rushed and clumsy rounds into another steamy vehicle, but both victims, twenty-year-old Sal Lup and seventeen-year-old Judy Placido, recovered from their injuries.

"We're hosting a very special event in Yonkers in a few

weeks," Robert said after the show, clasping Smoke's hand in both of his own. "We hope you and William will join us and grace our attendees with your wonderful song…"

CHAPTER ELEVEN

Out Go The Lights

The ringing in Vinny's ears went on-and-on, a droning scream.

"Get him the hell out of here! Take him back to the trailer, for fuck's sake!" Howard pointed and two Los Cappas came Vinny's way. Howard peeled off his jacket and dropped to one knee next to Vance's body. Blood pumped freely from the hole in Vance's head. Howard pressed his balled-up jacket against the wound with one hand, dialing his phone with the other. The Los Cappas lifted Vinny up, a seeming impossibility since they were much shorter, and carried him off stage.

"Vinny! What's going on?" Thom shouted. "Are you okay?"

"No!" Vinny shouted as the Los Cappas carried him away. "I'm pretty fucking far from okay!"

But the sound of Thom's forklift swallowed his words and Vinny sobbed openly and uncontrollably. The Los Cappas tossed him on the sofa in the trailer and left, slamming the door behind them. Vinny heard them talking outside. He didn't speak much Spanish, but he understood "hermano" and "muerte."

Christ, Vance! Why did you do it? How could you leave me to face this shit by myself, you bastard? Vinny was truly alone—no Pegdick, no crazy twin brother to care for. What happens now? Would Arkham assign him to another band, or would it finally release him, let him go home? What would he do if he got there? He couldn't imagine life without Vance.

Vinny staggered from the sofa to the bathroom. He puked in the toilet and searched the medicine cabinet, but found nothing stronger than aspirin. What happened to all their drugs? Vance's meds were still there, but not enough for an overdose. Two razors sat on the shelf in the shower, but they were cheap, disposable plastic. Vinny couldn't image how he'd slit his wrists with pivot-head, multi-blade action.

He splashed his face with water, went to the kitchen. He found the sharpest steak knife in the drawer and ran it across his wrist over the kitchen sink. It only chafed his skin, cutting off tiny white curls of flesh. It hurt too. Maybe he should run against the wall and impale the knife into his chest. He lit a cigarette to think about it and was still smoking thirty minutes later when Howard and another man arrived, carrying Vance between them.

"Vinny! Your brother's home!" Howard called, stepping into the trailer. "What are you doing with that knife, Vin? Put it down. Enough drama for one night, eh?"

Howard didn't need to tell Vinny twice. Vinny dropped the knife and ran to his brother, throwing his arms around him. Vance returned his brother's embrace, but it was awkward, like someone learning to hug for the first time.

Vinny studied his brother's face, the emptiness in Vance's eyes.

"Howard what the hell did you do?"

"I'll allow your brother's doctor to explain," Howard

said, nodding toward the other man in the room. "Dr. Umberto Corba, meet Arkham musician Vincent Boyle, Vance's brother."

"Pleased to meet you, Vinny," the doctor said, smiling and extending his hand. Corba was short, unassuming, and wore a jacket that had no chance of buttoning over his bulbous belly. "I'm a big fan of your music!"

Vinny ignored the handshake and hugged his brother again, twisting Vance around.

"What the hell did you do?" Vinny repeated, but he already knew. A surgical bandage covered the base of his brother's neck, another wrapped around the top of his skull.

"The bullet went in one temple and out the other, causing significant damage to your brother's frontal lobe," Howard said. "We had no choice but to use Arkham's unique assets to revive your brother. But thanks to Dr Corba's medical care, the majority of your brother's brain functions were saved. Doctor?"

"Well, yes, there was significant bleeding in both hemispheres, but we were able to cauterize most of the severed blood vessels." Dr. Corba pushed his thick-rimmed glasses up the bridge of his nose. "It was a hasty procedure, but given the conditions I'd say it was quite successful. Your brother will retain all of his lower brain functions, as well as higher cognitive skills like…"

Vinny released Vance and swung his fist at Howard's jaw. Howard stepped away and the blow glanced off his shoulder.

"Hey!" Howard shouted, stepping behind Vance. Vance's eyes followed Vinny, but he made no move to help his brother. "Vinny! Stop it! Your brother's been through a major physical trauma. We need to get him to bed. You too. We've all had a rough night. Please, call a truce. We can discuss things in the morning. Talk to your brother and sleep on it, Vinny. Please."

"Can he speak?" Vinny asked, staring at his twin brother as if seeing him for the first time.

"Light me a smoke, bro," Vance said.

"See there? Brotherly love!" Howard said. "Dr. Corba and I will help you get Vance out of these bloody clothes. Then it's beddy-bye for Vancy-pooh."

"I'll take care of him," Vinny said.

"We can help," Dr. Corba said. "If you'd like, I can show you how to change your brother's bandage."

"Get lost," Vinny said.

Howard scowled but shuffled out the door with Dr. Corba.

Vinny lit two cigarettes and handed one to his brother.

"Sit down," Vinny said. Vance lowered himself onto a kitchen chair. He puffed his cigarette, but didn't seem to inhale. Vinny perched on the sofa.

"This is fucked-up shit, bro," Vinny said.

"Yeah," Vance replied, watching the smoke swirl in the stale kitchen air. Vinny got up, switched on a vent fan, and sat back down. They both flicked their ashes on the floor.

"Are you really dead?"

"Do I look dead?" Vance asked.

"No," Vinny replied. "Does it hurt?"

"Not anymore," Vance said. His smile made Vinny uncomfortable.

"Let me help you get cleaned up," Vinny said. "You've got blood all over you."

"Don't sweat it." Vance kicked off his shoes and stood, tossing his cigarette into the sink. "Why is the steak knife out?"

"No reason," Vinny said. "You can put it back."

Vance put the knife back in the drawer. He unbuckled

his jeans and walked out of them on his way down the hall.

"I have a splitting headache," Vance said, easing himself into his bunk.

"You want something?" Vinny followed his brother into the bedroom. "We have aspirin."

"No, Doc Corba filled me full of all kinds of shit."

"Want to smoke a joint?"

"No."

"Something to drink? Water? Beer?"

"No, Vin."

"You going to sleep?"

"I don't think I need to," Vance said. "But I'll lay here with my eyes closed."

"Are you going to eat my face like Mom did to Dad?"

"No," Vance said. "I'm not hungry."

"What was it like being dead?" Vinny asked.

"I really don't remember," Vance said. "Quiet, I suppose."

"Quiet is good," Vinny said. "Silence is golden."

"It is," Vance said. "So why don't you pipe down and let me rest my head?"

"Okay, bro," Vinny said. "Let me know if you need anything."

Vance grunted and rolled over in his bunk to face the wall. He stayed that way, unmoving, unbreathing, until Howard and Dr. Corba arrived the following morning.

"How's our patient today?" Howard asked as he boarded the trailer, his voice filled with sunshine. "I trust everyone got a good night's sleep and woke rested and refreshed?"

"I don't think my brother needs to sleep anymore," Vinny said, watching Dr. Corba unwrap Vance's bandages. Two bloody wads of gauze plugged holes in his brother's temples, dime-sized on the right, a half-dollar on the left. Corba plucked the gauze out with tweezers and peered inside the wound with a flashlight. The light shone through Vance's skull and made a full moon on the opposite wall. Corba packed the wounds with fresh gauze and re-wrapped Vance's head.

"Did you sleep okay, Vinny?" Howard asked.

"Not a wink," Vinny said. "Is he going to eat my face off?"

"No. Don't be silly, Vin. What happened with your parents was an anomaly," Howard said. "Your brother retained much of his brain function. You have nothing to worry about."

"Can he still play?" Vinny asked.

"We'll find out," Howard said. "In the meantime, there's a band and crew meeting in fifteen minutes to discuss changes in our plans after last night's unfortunate events. I need you and your brother there."

"Whatever," Vinny said.

"Don't be difficult, Vincent," Howard said. "Just be there with your brother."

Howard and Dr. Corba left the trailer. Vance changed his bloody shirt and got himself dressed, even slicked his hair back and washed his face.

"How's your headache?" Vinny asked, watching his brother sit at the kitchen table and light a cigarette.

"Fine," Vance said. "Gone."

"You want something to eat?" Vinny asked. He slid a box of semi-stale doughnuts across the table to his brother. Vance took a doughnut out of the box and bit in, crumbs tumbling from his mouth as he chewed. He took drags off his cigarette between bites.

"Howard wants us at a band meeting in fifteen minutes," Vinny said.

"Whatever," Vance replied.

"He says it's important. Mandatory attendance."

"Fuck," Vance said. "Let's smoke a joint first."

They did, arriving a few minutes late. Only a handful of crew stood in a semi-circle around Howard. Thom sat on the back of his John Deere.

"Now that we're all here, I'd like to personally thank all of you, both new and old, for making this tour such a success."

Howard applauded and everyone joined in except Vinny.

"There are changes in our schedule, however, in light of recent events," Howard continued. "The upcoming Dunwich Horrors shows in Central America have been indefinitely postponed. As you can see, much of our crew has already been dismissed. Everyone will be paid the full amount agreed upon in their contracts. Those of you here today will be our core crew going forward on our next step."

"What's our next step?" Thom blurted out, sounding worried.

"The Dunwich Horrors have the unique opportunity to open for Allen Vent and The Strange Creations during the next leg of the band's tour," Howard said. A murmur of excitement bubbled through the crowd.

"'Midnight Tour' is everywhere!" Thom said. "Allen Vent is hot right now!"

"They blow," Vinny said. "'Midnight Tour' is pop-metal garbage."

A few people chuckled uncomfortably and Howard rolled his eyes.

"Despite your lack of support or respect, Vinny, Allen Vent and The Strange Creations have done quite well for themselves," Howard said. "An opening slot on their tour will bring your music to a much broader audience."

"Huge audiences!" Thom squealed. "They're a really good band."

"Didn't you hear my brother?" Vance said. "They blow."

"The musical abilities of your contemporaries is a topic for another time," Howard said. "Meanwhile, we rehearse, rehearse, rehearse, so we'll be in top form when we join The Strange Creations tour next week. I've procured rehearsal space across town, so we're staying in Panama City for a few days. I'm pleased to report we'll be moving to nicer accommodations at the Marriott near the marina and can check-in immediately, so gather your personal belongings, please."

"When is our first rehearsal?" Thom asked, as the crew dispersed.

"This afternoon," Howard said.

"I thought we had today off?" Vinny asked. "I thought we had the next *six* days off?"

"You have to strike while the iron is hot, Vincent!" Howard said. "The Allen Vent tour is a step up and we want to be prepared."

"We want to be rested, too. Wasn't that the plan?" Vinny asked. "Take time off…a limited number of shows per week. You told us this yesterday!"

Howard glanced around to make sure the rest of the crew was out of earshot before addressing Vinny. Thom leaned in close and the John Deere groaned beneath his bulk.

"That was the plan until your asshole brother used his head for target practice!" Howard hissed. "Corba and I did the best we could, but there is no guarantee your brother is going to perform at his previous skill level. And if he can't, you're screwed. Arkham will drop you. You don't want your band dropped by Arkham, Vinny. It's not pretty."

"I don't want to be dropped by Arkham!" Thom said. "I didn't do anything wrong!"

"Shut up, Thom! This isn't about you," Vinny said.

"Yeah, but I don't want Arkham to lump me in with you guys," Thom said.

"What's that supposed to mean?" Vinny said. "I thought you liked being in a band with us?"

"I do, but, you know, I don't want Arkham to penalize me for your behavior," Thom said. "I've got a signed contract with Arkham and I don't want to jeopardize it."

"Your brother had a signed contract too, fat boy," Vance said. "It doesn't mean shit."

"Gentlemen! Please! Remember yourselves!" Howard said. "This isn't a time for name-calling and in-fighting. It's time for the three of you to pull together and level up. These are the kinds of trials that make bands great! Channel that energy into the music!"

"How many other bands have members come back from the dead?" Vinny asked. "Except for Motley Crue."

"Don't get caught up in specifics, Vin," Howard said. "This is a turning point for your band. You can whine and cry and wring your hands like little boys, or you can rise up and play like men!"

"I'm not sure I can play anything anymore," Vance said.

"How's your head, man?" Thom asked.

"Strange," Vance said.

"That's normal for you," Vinny said.

"Different strange," Vance said. "But, yeah. I guess."

"We won't know how well you can play until we rehearse, Vance," Howard said. "Can I give you a ride to the studio?"

Vinny drove Vance to the studio himself, in a sweet Mustang rented by Arkham. Howard traveled in the transit van with Thom. They rehearsed in a rusty warehouse just outside the city limits. It looked abandoned and overrun by palm trees, but the inside was clean and brightly lit. Their equipment was arranged in a semi-circle in the middle of the room.

Vance did his best, and, though Vinny was impressed, it was clear Vance was not the man he used to be behind the piano.

"You may need to take over on keyboards, Vinny," Howard said during a break. "Let Vance handle the bass parts….maybe transcribe them for oboe."

"Let my brother try again tomorrow," Vinny said.

Howard allowed it, but Vance didn't improve. He played with skill and precision, but it lacked the emotion that once made his playing so accomplished. They tried "The Summoning Song" three times, but the best they could produce was wavy air.

"Howard wants me to take over your keyboard parts," Vinny told his brother while they smoked and watched tiny lizards with red gobblers dart up and down the palm trees. Vance shrugged.

"Do you care?" Vinny asked.

"Nope," his brother said. The wounds at Vance's temples oozed pink through the bandages.

"Do you care about anything?"

"Nope," Vance said, lighting another smoke. "Sorry, Vin, but not really. No."

"Do you wish you were still dead?"

"I don't think so," Vance said. "Life's cool. Death. Whatever."

Vinny played keyboards after the break, but it was shaky. Vance's parts were hard. "The Summoning Song" didn't even shimmer.

"It'll get better," Howard said. "Give it time and find the core energy of the piece, gentlemen."

Things sucked for three days, but by Thursday "The Summoning Song" smoked. They spent the bulk of rehearsal transposing parts to other instruments. Vance got the song cooking with oboe and violin, even if he no longer could with the piano. Vinny improved on the keyboards and found, with a few tuning tweaks, many of the parts could be played on six-string bass, freeing his brother up to experiment. By Friday the warehouse dripped with terrible, liquid shadows and a hole with teeth appeared in the middle of the floor.

"Gentlemen, I think you're ready to hit the road with Allen Vent and The Strange Creations!" Howard said. The hole in the floor gnashed its teeth in agreement.

CHAPTER TWELVE

Creatures Of Love

The Dunwich Horrors met The Strange Creations at a corporate lounge in JFK Airport in New York City, another Arkham-approved, dark-paneled private meeting place. Everyone shook hands as Howard made introductions.

Allen Vent ignored the Boyle brothers beyond a limp handshake, but hit it off with Thom Thomas. They shared an interest in wizarding and witchcraft. (Thom slightly disappointed to hear Allen was only Level 5.)

"Dig the band name," Allen said, and Thom rattled off a bunch of gobbly-gook names that struck a nerve with Allen.

"Hey, you know my bosses!" Allen laughed, making Thom and Howard laugh too.

"This is a fucking dork-fest," Vinny said to Vance, but his brother didn't reply. Vance watched planes roll around the tarmac outside the window.

Everybody boarded a private jet half-an-hour later, Thom forklifted into the back— his own "first class cargo hold," Howard called it. Allen Vent sat by Howard on the plane, Howard's laptop open, Allen referring to a messy notebook filled with scratches and scrawls. The rest of the

Strange Creations spread about the plane. Nobody socialized, but Vinny spent a few minutes with each member of the band. *We're touring Asia together for the next month. Might as well start out on good terms.*

Bassist Bobby Marks told Vinny to go away. Mick and Ritchie, the drummer and guitarist, were friendlier, though Ritchie's sallow skin and vacant eyes gave Vinny the willies. Vinny lived with Pegdick long enough to spot a junkie. Ritchie asked about The Horrors' music, but fell silent and didn't listen to the answer. Mick picked up the conversation like a deftly recovered fumble, launching into dissertations on equipment, musical influences, and the sensual qualities of Asian women.

"Chinky chicks love tall, skinny fucks like you and your brother," Mick said. "You guys gonna be balls-deep in Jap gash the next three weeks!"

The idea intrigued Vinny, but his brother showed no response. Vance showed no interest in sex since his reanimation. He showed no interest in anything, except smoking cigarettes and pot. He didn't take his medication any longer.

"Cured, bro," Vance said when Vinny asked. Vance's temples scabbed over, though sometimes he scratched them until they bled. The itch must be maddening.

Three hours into the flight, Howard summoned Vinny up front to sit beside him and Allen Vent.

"We need your support on this tour, Vinny," Howard flashed his shitty shark-tooth smile. "And not just as an opening act."

"We're all working together to open the Infinitus," Allen said. "And you know the importance of blood sacrifice."

"Why me?" Vinny asked. "Didn't we bring any Los Cappas with us?"

"Not this time, Vin," Howard said. "Surprisingly, not

many Los Cappas had valid passports...or verifiable identities."

"You understand the Lament of Chaugnar Faugn, the Sorrow of Nug and Yeb," Allen said. "Howard said Rhan-Tegoth appeared at your show. That's fantastic!"

"Is he the one with the claws or the tentacles?" Vinny asked.

Allen gave him a long, strange look.

"Claws," he said, turning to Howard. "Who showed with tentacles? The *big guy*?"

Howard raised his eyebrows, but changed the topic.

"Allen and his band are close to making something very exciting happen," Howard said. "It's important Allen have access to the raw material he needs for the rituals he's performing."

"The Mouth of Despair...The Arabat of Hypnos..." Allen continued as if Vinny understood or cared.

"You play 'The Summoning Song' too?" Vinny asked.

Allen looked puzzled.

"'Hangman's Jam?'" he asked. His eyes narrowed, and he stared into Vinny's face. "Do you know Smoke Johnson?"

"Who?"

"Same song, vastly different arrangements," Howard interjected. "The gang at Arkham believe Allen Vent and The Strange Creations are in a better position, at this time, to bring the song to its fullest potential and functionality. As such, The Dunwich Horrors will put their full support behind Allen and the boys."

"You want us to...kill for the band?" Vinny asked, but Allen shouted over him.

"This is your Plan B, Howie?" Allen said. "Get an opening act to play the song instead of us? This is what Arkham calls putting faith in our group?"

"There's nothing wrong with a backup plan, Allen," Howard tried his shark-smile, but Allen wanted none of it. "Give The Horrors a chance. I'm sure you'll be impressed with the musical skills of Thom Thomas and the Boyle brothers. Vinny can play circles around Bobby on bass. Arkham felt it a good idea to have other musicians familiar with the Infinitus on the tour...just in case. It's not a lack of faith in your band, Allen, it's an insurance policy Arkham insisted on."

Vinny took a deep breath. *Smell the pizza...blow out the candles...*

"The other morning at breakfast, William Deacon Jr. called us the most talented band on Arkham's roster," he said. "He called Thom Thomas a force of nature, said we connected with the song on a primal level. Was he lying?"

Howard turned hot pink, Allen bright red.

"Those statements were made before your brother blew a chunk of his brain out," Howard replied. "Maybe you *were* the best band, but not now, not without your brother's former skills. He always was the more talented twin. I'm sure you know that, right, Vin? Your brother *felt* the music, played with soul and emotion. With you it's more of a paint-by-numbers job."

Speechless, Vinny nodded. Allen looked at the floor. *He's ashamed for me*, Vinny realized, which made him feel even more ashamed.

"We're all impressed with how you've stepped up to fill your brother's shoes, Vinny, but it is simply not enough," Howard said. "Your primary responsibilities are to perform a thirty-minute opening set, be ready if you are needed to sit in with The Strange Creations, and assist Allen Vent with his occult work. Is that understood?"

"What about my brother?" Vinny asked.

"Yes, and care for your brother, of course," Howard

said. "You'll no doubt find it easier now that his mental disorders are resolved."

"No, I mean, what is Vance going to do?" Vinny asked. "What are his responsibilities?"

"Play for thirty minutes and do whatever you or Allen tell him to," Howard said, turning to Allen. "Brief Vincent on the tasks you'll need him to perform in Asia."

Allen made a laundry list of absurd items: potions, crystals, spices, body parts…

"Thom is your man for this," Vinny said. "He understands all this witchy stuff. Not me."

"You're correct," Howard said. "Thom is better suited for the job in many ways. For starters, he'd be honored to do it. But Thom has mobility issues and your brother has psychological issues. That leaves you, Vinny. I believe in you personally and professionally. You can do this!"

"Excuse me," Vinny said. He turned away from Howard and Allen's shocked faces and returned to the rear of the plane. *Shove your pep talk up your ass, Howard.*

Vinny hunkered next to his brother. Vance stared out the window, even though the dark of night showed nothing besides wing lights and his own reflection. Vinny waited for Vance to ask how the meeting went. Old Vance would have known it sucked from the look on Vinny's face.

"That meeting was fucked up, Vance," Vinny finally said.

"How so?" Vance asked without looking away from the window.

"They want us to kill for Allen Vent," Vinny said, nearly laughing because the statement sounded so ridiculous spoken aloud. "Evidently The Strange Creations do blood sacrifices too."

"Wow. Okay," Vance said, looking away from the window at last, his expression blank. "Are we still the opening act?"

"Yeah, but no 'Summoning Song,'" Vinny said. "Howard says The Strange Creations do a better version."

"Bummer," Vance said.

Vinny shook his head. "Vance, we have to get out of this. We can't kill people! We're not murderers!"

Vance thought for a long moment.

"Haven't people died and gotten eaten and whatnot at our shows for the past year?" Vance said. "I didn't imagine that, right?"

"Yes."

"So, technically we're already murderers…"

"No! We're musicians!" Vinny said. "Okay…maybe *accessories* since we're playing the song…but we're not killing people with our bare hands!"

"Is that what Howard asked you to do?"

"No…but he wants us to supply 'raw materials' for Allen's rituals," Vinny said. "What does that sound like to you?"

"Maybe we can do it from a distance," Vance said. "Keep our bare hands clean."

"Is that what we are, Vance?" Vinny asked. "Murderers? Cold-blooded killers? Christ, what have we become?"

"We do what we have to, Vin, like we always do," Vance said. "We get by. Do you want me to talk to Howard? Get specifics?"

"No. No, Vance," Vinny said. "Let's…let's sit here for a minute, okay, bro? I need to…just chill…"

Vance looked out the window again.

"If we don't do this, what do we do?" Vance asked.

"I don't know, man," Vinny rubbed his chest. "Maybe hop a flight back home and join a wedding band."

"I look good in a tux," Vance said. He pointed to his scabby temples. "Might need a hat. Maybe a wig."

"Santana bandana," Vinny said, his voice tight. "You could pull it off. Or a do-rag like Little Steven."

"Yeah," Vance said.

"Shit, Vance, I think I'm having a heart attack." Cold sweat broke out all over Vinny's body. His hearing went tinny, heart pounding in his chest.

"No," Vance said. "You're having a panic attack, Vin."

"How do you know?"

"I used to get them all the time," Vance said. "Hold my hand."

Vinny welcomed Vance's cold, lifeless hand. He squeezed and Vance squeezed back. *We haven't held hands since we were kids*. Vinny hadn't been this scared since childhood either, back when monsters were mere shadows cast on bedroom walls and Vance could whisper reassurances that chased away the darkness.

"Smell the pizza, Vinny," Vance said. "Blow out the candles."

Vinny followed his brother's advice until his pounding heart slowed. Vance sang "Yesterday" and Vinny joined him the second time around. But the question wouldn't stop knocking around Vinny's head.

What have we become, Vance? What have we become?

Maybe his dead brother was the wrong person to ask, but he was all Vinny had.

CHAPTER THIRTEEN

The Zoo

"Shit, Vance! Look at the size of this place!"

Standing in the center of Shanghai's Grand Stage, looking out at the ornate, empty theater, Vinny's bowels trembled. "How many seats does this place have?"

"Eleven thousand," Howard said. "And every one will be filled tonight. Well, not for the opening act…half-filled for you."

"Wow," Vance said, looking around the vast space, sounding unimpressed.

"Don't worry, boys," Howard said. "It'll be a great show. Get out there and have fun!"

They did. Vance tore up the violin with a passion Vinny rarely heard from his brother. They debuted a new song, "Curmudgeon," featuring Vinny on electric guitar. Compared to his six-string bass, the Les Paul was a tiny toy, but Vinny appreciated its chordal possibilities. Vance switched between saxophone and oboe, laying down wild melodies over Thom's frenetic beat.

They got a good round of applause when their set finished. Only Thom was disappointed.

"Why can't we play The Infinitus?" he whined. A three-man crew navigated a forklift to hoist him off the drum riser. "It's not fair!"

"We sounded great tonight, Thom," Vance said. "Don't sweat it."

"It's not fair!" Thom repeated, glaring at the Boyle brothers. "If *you* two hadn't screwed everything up, we'd be headliners right now instead of an opening act!"

"So lose four hundred pounds and join another band," Vinny suggested. "Or find another band with a forklift."

Thom scowled.

"I have a signed contract with Arkham..." he muttered.

"Yeah, yeah, don't we all," Vinny said. A twenty-man crew swept their instruments off stage and set up The Strange Creations' gear. *This is all Arkham. We're all slaves to the corporate beast. But who does the beast serve?*

"We got bosses too, and if you think *we're* assholes, you should meet *her*!" William Deacon Jr. had laughed over his airport breakfast, but Vinny couldn't imagine anything worse than this...until Allen asked the Boyles to meet him backstage before the encore. Two hours and ten minutes later, Vinny and Vance waited at the bottom of the stage stairs. Allen hopped down, dripping sweat, radiating the manic energy of an artist in mid-performance.

"Section A, Row C, seats four and five," he said. "Section C, Row B, one through six."

"What?" Vinny said.

"For after the show," Allen said.

Vance understood.

"Section A, Row C, seats four and five. Section C, Row B, one through six," Vance repeated.

Allen nodded and returned to the stage.

"Get the people in A," Vance told his brother. "I'll take care of Section C."

The two girls in Section A didn't speak English, but recognized Vinny from the opening act. They nodded eagerly when he asked, "Do you want to party with Allen after the show?" He escorted the girls to Allen's dressing room. Vance waited with a boisterous group; two skinny men, and four more young girls. Very young.

"Yeah! Yeah! Allen Vent! Strange Creations!" exhausted their English vocabulary, but it was enough. Allen showed up sweaty and smiling ten minutes later and Vinny and Vance quietly slipped out of the room.

"What do we do now?" Vinny asked.

"Smoke," Vance said, lighting a cigarette. All of Vance's addictive behaviors stopped post-mortem except for nicotine. *Even death can't kill the craving*, Vinny thought. *Smokes are a bitch*. He lit up too.

"Are we supposed to wait by Allen's dressing room?" Vinny asked, exhaling a blue plume.

"No," Vance said, walking toward the exit. "He'll let us know." The Horrors didn't have dressing rooms, but their tour bus waited outside. Thom got his own van.

Allen texted Vinny at five the next morning.

"Come."

Vinny smelled blood and shit wafting from Allen's dressing room before he opened the door.

"Wow," Vance said, as unimpressed by the bloody mess as he was by Shanghai's Grand Stage. Allen sat cross-legged on the floor, inside a hand-drawn circle. Other drawings, some in blood, others in charcoal, sprawled across the floor, strange shapes, squiggles, stickmen, stickwomen, stickmonsters, telling a story Vinny couldn't fathom. A hunk of burnt meat smoldered on a gold plate. It smelled minty and acrid and Vinny covered his lower face with his t-shirt.

"Take her away," Allen pointed to a body in the corner

of the dressing room, its chest torn open. "There's tarp on the sofa. Corba will meet you by the freight entrance."

"Dr. Corba's here?" Vinny asked, unsure why this was his first question.

"Of course." Allen sounded frustrated, exhausted.

Vance unfolded the tarp and the brothers rolled the girl's corpse in plastic. Vinny didn't look at her face, hoped she wasn't a Section A girl. Vinny thought Allen fell asleep until he muttered, "Thanks," on their way out.

"Yep," Vance said, closing the door behind him.

They each carried an end of the tarp.

"Christ, Vance! This is so fucked up!" Vinny said. "Allen *killed* this girl! Tore her apart like an animal!"

"Yep," Vance said.

"It's not cool, Vance! It's wrong!" Vinny said. "We're not murderers, man!"

"Not really," Vance agreed. "Not yet."

"I don't want to go there, Vance," Vinny said. "We have to get out of here."

"What do you suggest?"

"I don't know."

"Then why don't we follow orders until you figure it out?" Vance suggested.

Dr. Corba waited at the freight entrance with an ambulance.

"Good to see you again, gentlemen!" Corba helped them lift the tarp onto a stretcher and slide it into the back of the ambulance. He inspected the wounds on Vance's temples.

"Healing nicely!" he proclaimed, bidding them goodnight and driving off into the sunrise, another Arkham force of nature.

"This is fucked, Vance," Vinny repeated.

"Yep," Vance agreed.

"How can we get out of this?" Vinny felt lost and

scared, close to tears.

"Ritchie Smith," Vance said. "He's a drug addict. A weak link."

Vinny looked at his brother.

"Yeah?"

"Yep," Vance said.

Two nights later, Ritchie Smith played the Tokyo Dome. Drug addict or no, Ritchie played with amazing feel and expression, though Vinny found him too flashy. *Fucking rock star*, Vinny thought, watching Ritchie windmill his Les Paul and mug for the crowd.

Ritchie came out of a guitar solo into a blistering opening run, doubling Allen on the keyboard. The arena erupted with cheers and screams. The whole band kicked in and the Dome pulsed in time with the music, temperature rising, black slime dripping from the rafters, shadowy figures appearing among the crowd, walking *atop* the crowd, as an elephant covered with blinking, weeping boils unfurled an impossibly long trunk stretching nearly to the roof, the waving arms of the audience indistinguishable from the wriggling flagella of an enormous, single-celled creature. The song went on-and-on...even when Vinny covered his ears it seeped through his fingers into his brain. *Damn, this is how "The Summoning Song" was* meant *to be played!* Ritchie Smith's fingers scaled the fretboard like tiny gymnasts. *I can't do that...I don't want to do that...* Vinny wanted to tear his ears off, the song was so awful, so terrible, so beautiful.

"Awesome!" Vance applauded as The Strange Creations wrapped up. The menacing shadows faded. "These guys are fucking good!"

"You're nuts, bro," Vinny looked at his brother like he had two heads.

"Not so much," Vance replied. "Not anymore."

Allen waved them behind the drum riser, pointing out tonight's invitees. Vinny clapped Ritchie on the shoulder before wading into the audience to harvest Allen's catch.

"You're an amazing player, man," Vinny said.

"Thanks," Ritchie said. He looked ready to fall over. *Will he make it through the encore?*

"Hey, man, you want to get happy after the show?" Vinny said. "My brother and I can get you anything you want."

"Cool. Thanks," Ritchie said. "I usually cop from Randy…our roadie."

"I'll talk to him," Vinny said. "Have a great encore."

"Yeah," Ritchie said. "Thanks again."

Vinny spoke with Randy after collecting Allen's "lucky" fans. *More teens in schoolgirl uniforms. Guy's a fucking pedo as well as a ritualist killer.* Randy acted coy when Vinny offered him drugs.

"No worries, man," Randy said. "Arkham provides."

What? The same company pushing Ritchie to play, also helped him kill himself? Arkham must want Ritchie compliant and malleable, just shy of dead.

Allen summoned them before dawn. Another dead girl lie crumpled in the corner, chest torn apart. But another girl was still alive, a crude gash in her side seeping blood. She moaned, lacking the strength to scream when Vance tried to move her.

"Please…please…" she said in broken English. "He cut something from me…"

Allen gave no instruction, brooding silently before his smoking plate of minty meat. *What the hell* is *that?*

"Corba will know what to do," Vance said.

They wrapped the dead girl in plastic. Vance slung her over his shoulder, grabbing the injured girl's feet. He helped Vance carry her to the freight entrance, covering her in blankets so she didn't drip.

Vance laid the dead girl inside Dr. Corba's ambulance. The doctor made no attempt to treat the injured girl.

"Oh dear," he said, parting the wound in the girl's side with gloved hands. The girl found the strength to scream— once, short and shrill. "She might survive without a kidney, but not a liver. I'm afraid she's done."

He stepped back and snapped off his rubber gloves, looking at Vinny and Vance.

"What?" Vinny said.

"You have to extinguish her," Dr Corba said.

"Please…" the girl moaned.

"See? She agrees," Corba said. "Put her out of her misery."

"You're a doctor," Vinny said. "Don't you have a shot or something in the ambulance you can give her?"

"I took an oath!" Corba said. "First, do no harm!"

"Give me a fucking break!" Vinny said, but before he could protest further, Vance pinched the girl's nose shut and covered her mouth with his palm. Her cheeks bellowed out around his hand, a panicked look in her eyes.

"*Shh*," Vance whispered, as soft and sweet as a lover. "*Shh, baby.* You're going to be okay."

The light in the girl's eyes dimmed until Vinny stared at dead meat.

"Christ, Vance," Vinny said. "What have you done?"

"I did what she wanted," Vance said.

"She didn't want to die!" Vinny said. "She wanted our help!"

"She was beyond help!" Dr. Corba chided. "Your brother did what he needed to do. He did his job."

"This isn't our job!" Vinny said. "We're musicians!"

"And I'm a brain surgeon," Dr. Corba smirked. "Sometimes life has other plans for us, Vin."

CHAPTER FOURTEEN
Black Magic Woman

Evita Swallows was Bobby's porn star girlfriend from Las Vegas to California, down the West Coast of the United States, and through most of Europe. By the time they arrived back in the United States, Evita was Allen's girlfriend. Everyone on the crew enjoyed time with Evita Swallows, but Vinny was particularly smitten. Everything about Evita was magical to Vinny, her voice, her eyelashes, the way she tossed her hair to the side when she spoke, and the way she ground cigarette butts beneath her spiked heels. Evita captivated Vinny.

"Allen and I have a modern arrangement," Evita told Vinny one night, straddling him in the back of Arkham's private jet, the others only a few rows away, her skirt hiked up around her hips, her Czech accent thick, her laugh throaty. She drove Vinny to heights of ecstasy he'd never experienced. He knew it was foolish, but he felt himself falling in love with her.

Allen grew ambivalent toward Evita after a few months. Vinny would have made a serious play for her if Evita didn't insist on sexually servicing the rest of the crew, including crawling between Thom Thomas' beefy thighs night after night. The thought filled Vinny with an odd combination of disgust and relief. Thom was a bear when he didn't "get his nut."

Evita kept everyone satisfied. Vance called her "the Florence Nightingale of boners," but, to Vinny, she was an angel on earth.

"You're letting your dick do the thinking," Vance told him during a bus ride from Exeter to Concord, sunlight setting the autumn leaves ablaze. "You're not in love with her. She fucks you and she's nice to you, so you think you're supposed to love her. Don't get your heart broken, Vin."

"You never slept with her," Vinny said. "She…she could make a dead man cum, Vance."

"Funny, Vin," Vance said.

Evita devoted herself to "The Great Work" and her belief in an impending "Dawn Of Reclamation." She danced in the wings when Allen Vent and The Strange Creations played their version of "The Summoning Song." She connected with the music on an otherworldly level, and the terrifying shadows, shapes, and creatures moved and swayed with Evita as if they were one-and-the-same. Watching Evita dance with demons thrilled Vinny. It was so hypnotic and beautiful, alluring and repellent, hideous and harmonizing.

Vinny couldn't master Ritchie Smith's guitar parts. He tried to follow Ritchie's fingers and Vinny *thought* he understood, but he simply couldn't make his fingers mimic Ritchie's. Vinny played until his calloused fingertips blistered, but it was too fast, too complicated.

"Keep trying," Evita encouraged him. "You may be called upon to play a very important role. You want to be ready when the time comes."

"I'm peaking out," Vinny said, setting his Les Paul aside. "I'm as good as I'm going to get and I'm still not good enough."

"Then try harder!" Evita said. "The Infinitus won't be kept waiting. Don't you understand the importance of The Great Work?"

"Not really," Vinny admitted. "It has something to do with opening a doorway so monsters can take over the world."

"It's about ridding this world of the pestilence of humanity!" Evita was truly passionate, which made Vinny realize how much she faked passion during intercourse. "It's about opening a doorway so *gods* can *reclaim* what is *rightfully theirs*!"

"What happens then?" Vinny asked. "We become food for the gods, like the H.G. Wells story?"

"Most of humanity will be destroyed in the first wave of The Reclamation," Evita said. "What remains will be enslaved. Slaves need masters. That's what's promised to us, Vinny. We become masters of the new world! Either that, or we take the rocket ship to Uranus."

"Are you talking about…anal sex?" Vinny asked.

"You stupid man. The Deacons have procured passage to the moons of Uranus. Titania, Miranda, Unbridle, Ariel, Oberon…the Great Old Ones dwelt there for millennia," Evita said. "We will be kept safe until the Old Ones deem it time for us to return to earth."

"Are you crazy?" Vinny said and immediately regretted it. Evita's wide-eyed glare and flared nostrils made her look as mad as a hatter. "People can't survive on the moons of Uranus. It's not possible. The Deacons are lying to you."

"You don't know what's possible,Vincent," Evita said, uttering his name like a curse. "You spend so much time taking care of your eunuch brother, you miss what's happening right in front of you."

"There's no rocket ship to Uranus, Evita," Vinny said. "I'm sorry."

"Don't be a fool, Vinny. Open your little mind up," Evita said. She picked up the Les Paul and tossed it in his lap. "And practice your damn guitar!"

"I will," Vinny said. "But I'm telling you, I'll never be Ritchie Smith."

"Be your own goddamn man!" Evita said. She reached beneath the Les Paul and gave his testicles a not-so-playful tug. "Use your *balls*, Vinny! The new world needs masters!"

"I'm more of a baiter," Vinny said, but Evita either failed to get his dumb joke, or willfully ignored it.

"You're more of a dunderhead," Evita said. "Have faith, Vinny. With an open heart and mind, anything is possible."

Later, when Vinny retold the story to Vance, his brother howled with laughter.

"Sounds like she's with the Church of Latter Day Saints!" Vance said. "A rocketship to Uranus! That's a punchline to a dirty joke!"

"Yeah," Vinny said, but watching Vance scratch the fresh pink skin around his temples, Vinny wasn't sure what was possible anymore, couldn't differentiate reality from illusion, or a dirty joke from a cosmic truth.

Allen Vent and The Strange Creations played Tampa Bay and monsters rose from the Gulf, black-winged nightmares filling the air, ghosts, swirling, twisting, twirling, alive again. *Damn, when Allen and Ritchie get going, the song is unstoppable!* The Strange Creations played with a fire and passion Vinny and his brother lacked. The night bloomed with living shadows.

Evita shimmied ecstatically on the side of the stage, a black horseshoe crab with red, stalked eyes and the curved, segmented tail of a scorpion scurrying around her feet. Her moves entranced Vinny…until Howard laid a hand on his shoulder, breaking the spell.

"Vinny, can we have a moment," Howard said. The Deacons stood behind Howard. William Jr. offered a close-lipped smile, William Sr. expressionless.

"Sure," Vinny said. He followed Howard and the Deacons to an empty, concrete-walled cafeteria in the basement of Raymond James Stadium, feeling underdressed and childlike in his jeans and t-shirt. They sat at a long lunch table, the Deacons on one side, Vinny and Howard on the other, furthering the impression Vinny was back in grade school, seated at the teachers' table.

"I'll cut to the chase, Vin," Howard said. "We have concerns about Allen Vent and The Strange Creations' ability to open the Infinitus."

"They looked pretty close tonight," Vinny said. "They were killing it out there. Literally."

Howard shook his head.

"They certainly cause a spectacle, but I didn't see Rhan-Tegoth show up, did you?" Howard gave Vinny a sly wink. It felt like insects crawling on his skin.

"There are a couple of factors at play here," William Jr. said. "First, the song takes a physical and emotional toll on those who play it, as you know."

Yes, I know. It made my brother kill himself.

"We have concerns about how Allen and the other band members are holding up under the rigors of touring," William Jr. said.

"It's Ritchie Smith," Howard said. "You may have noticed he has a serious substance abuse problem. Ritchie is in very poor health and needs to get to rehab. Instead of cancelling shows we're hoping you can fill in for him."

"Guys, I'm sorry," Vinny said. "I've practiced day-and-night, but I simply can't play guitar like Ritchie."

"But you play the song on the bass guitar," William Jr. said.

"Yes, but a standard scale guitar has an entirely different feel," Vinny said. *It's not that I* can't *play the song on guitar...I can't tap into that space where the song plays itself.*

William Sr. shook his head.

"Different scale...different timbre...won't work," he said. "Maybe try a baritone neck and split the difference."

"Or run Vinny's bass through an octave pedal," William Jr. suggested.

"I know the tech manager for Royal Blood," Howard said. "I'll get in touch and see how they do it."

"Worth a try," William Sr. said. "In the meantime, what other instruments do you play, Vincent?"

"Viola," Vinny said. "Keyboards a bit."

"Vincent is being modest. He's a very accomplished keyboardist," Howard said. "I had the honor of awarding him the first place ribbon at a Chancellor Academy piano recital back when he was just a boy. Do you remember, Vin?"

Vinny nodded and William Jr. offered a bland, disinterested smile.

"Do you know Smoke Johnson?" William Jr. asked.

A thousand dirty jokes raced across Vinny's mind, but he opted for the truth.

"Allen mentioned his name once," Vinny said. "Other than that, I've never heard of him."

"Smoke played the blues," William Sr. said. "Spread our tune through the music industry like a whore spreads crabs through a barracks. Been after him for years...and we finally got him."

"Smoke Johnson recently signed a contract with Arkham Records after decades of negotiations," William Jr.

explained. "Smoke's first assignment will be teaming up with you and your brother."

"Smoke'll show you how to stroke those keys and make the night dance, that's for sure," William Sr. chuckled. "Get Smoke and Allen, you don't need Ritchie. It's the timbre, I'm telling you…it's got to blend…"

"We believe after a few private workshops with Smoke Johnson, you and your brother will be ready to take over for Ritchie Smith without having to play guitar," William Jr. said.

"I'm not sure I understand," Vinny said. "Why doesn't Smoke Johnson fill in for Ritchie?"

"Smoke is quite old," Howard said. "And there are other…physical limitations preventing Smoke Johnson from touring."

Christ, Howard found another five-hundred-pound band member! Hope Arkham has another forklift!

"Meet with Smoke. Learn from him," William Jr. intoned. "I promise you, Smoke is a character you won't forget!"

CHAPTER FIFTEEN
She's Come Undone

Oppressive heat beat down on San Antonio, TX like a fist, but the dressing rooms beneath Alamo Stadium were a few degrees cooler. Vinny practiced guitar. Even though the new plan had him playing keyboards, he still tried to master Ritchie Smith's parts. He'd feel like a failure otherwise.

Evita entered, wearing a long, flowing gown, neckline plunging to her navel, a schoolboy's wet dream prom date.

"Evita…you're so beautiful," Vinny told her.

Evita blushed, her eyes wet. *Was she crying?* Must be the glare from the overhead fluorescents.

"I like the way I feel when you look at me, Vinny," Evita said. "You think you see the real me, but you don't. Thank you for looking at me the way you do, Vinny. It's one of the things I love most about you."

Vinny's heart leapt in his chest.

"I…I love you too!" he blurted out.

Evita laughed.

"Have a good show, Vincent." She left the dressing room so quickly, the bottom of her ball gown cracked like a whip.

The room deflated, as if Evita took all the good vibes with her. Did she really love Vinny? Maybe she left so suddenly because she was overcome with emotion and couldn't face the depth of her feelings for him. Vinny should have taken her in his arms, told her everything would work out. They would leave this terrible tour, live on an island, someplace warm, sunny, trouble-free. Why didn't he do that?

Vance arrived fifteen minutes before showtime.

"You alright?" he asked Vinny. "You look like shit."

"I'm okay," Vinny said. "A little out of it."

"This joint should help." Vance pulled one from his cigarette pack and lit up. The paper end flamed for a second before Vance toked the marijuana to life. He passed it to Vinny, who sucked on it greedily.

"Gonna be hot as balls on stage," Vance said. "Make sure you drink water, okay?"

"Yes, mother," Vinny replied, coughing into his fist. "*Fucker!*"

"Don't make me Pegdick you," Vance said. "Take care of yourself, Vinny."

"Okay."

It was hot as balls on stage. Vinny felt like he might pass out fifteen minutes into their set. His playing was marginal, tentative, but Vance spread out and explored new musical textures, adding a yodeling coda to "Lucille," and taking an extended violin solo in "Curmudgeon." Thom drove the beat like a tank, accentuating Vance's experimental playing with Keith Moon-like drum fills. Thom scowled whenever he looked at Vinny. *What the hell is wrong with you?* written large on Thom's sweaty, pudgy face.

Their set ended with a smattering of applause. Vinny staggered off stage and poured a bottle of Poland Spring over his head, shaking the water clear.

"Easy, Lassie," Vance said, shielding his face with his forearms. He clapped Vinny on the back. "Good show! I played amazing and you played like shit. You sure you're okay?"

"Yeah, but I need to get back to the bus where it's air-conditioned," Vinny said. They both moved aside to make way for Thom's forklift.

"Great show, guys!" Thom called down from his drum riser, but Vance and Vinny walked away and didn't turn back.

"Are you lovesick?" Vance asked.

"No!" Vinny said.

"I told you she'd break your heart, Vinny."

"I'm not..." The words stuck in Vinny's throat. He swallowed a ball of thumbtacks and tried again. "I'm not."

"Sure, bro," Vance said. "Let's cool down. This is nothing a fat joint can't fix."

"Pot doesn't cure everything," Vinny said. "It doesn't cure *anything*."

"You're wrong there, brother." Vance held the exit door open for Vinny. "It's good medicine."

"Do you still get high?" Vinny asked.

"Not really," Vance said. "But sometimes, when I smoke a lot, it helps me forget I'm dead inside."

The air-conditioned bus was a blessed relief from the Texas heat, but Vinny didn't get to enjoy it long. Halfway through The Strange Creations' set, all the crew members fled their buses and ran toward the stage.

"Let's see what's going on, bro," Vance said. Vinny followed him back into Alamo Stadium.

A body swung from the lighting rig two stories above the stage. Fire burned below it. Two crew members with extinguishers ran past the Boyles up the stage steps.

"Did a pyro effect explode?" Vance pointed to the stage

as they walked closer. The swinging body whooshed back and forth like a pendulum through the fire. "Is that supposed to happen?"

Its elegant gown ignited, and the body swung like a flaming pendulum.

"Evita!" Vinny cried. He sprinted toward the stage, nearly colliding with Howard, who guided Ritchie Smith and Mick the Stick toward the exit, like a school principal taking behavioral students to his office.

"Vinny! Vance!" Howard shouted over his shoulder as he hurried past. "We need to get out of here. Get back on your bus, please."

Vinny ignored him and plowed toward the stage. *Christ, Evita!* Somebody snipped the wire atop the lighting rig, and the burning body tumbled to the stage. Two men with fire extinguishers obliterated the scene in a cloud of white foam.

"This looks fucked," Vance said, coming up behind his brother. Vinny searched the crew, hoping to spot Evita in the wings. The body above the stage couldn't be her. This was their chance…their getaway…their tropical island…

"She's not here, Vin. She's…gone," Vance said, nodding toward the smoky cloud on stage. "I'm sorry."

The crew cleared the stage so quickly, it looked like a time-lapse video. Scaffolding came down, instruments packed away, the atmosphere manic but controlled, crazed but efficient, the Arkham way.

Allen emerged from the smoky stage. He looked dazed, cradling something in his arms.

"Allen!" Vance called out. "Do you need help?"

Allen shook his head, bleached hair sweaty, sooty, and speckled with fire-retardant foam. He hunched over, as if protecting something in his arms.

"Corba. Bus," Allen said, eyes down as he hurried past.

"Did Allen rescue a kitten from the fire?" Vance asked. "That's so sweet...and great PR."

Where was Evita? Crew members carried a smoking stretcher off stage. Vinny looked around, confused. Not long ago, he couldn't imagine leaving Vance behind. Now he couldn't think of anything worse than spending the rest of his life with his half-dead brother.

"Come on, Vinny." Vance laid his hand on Vinny's back, guiding him toward the exit. "You heard the boss. Corba. Bus."

Corba waited next to a coroner's van parked behind Allen's bus, the stretcher beside him. Corba pulled the sheet away and Vinny recognized the barbed-wire tattoo around the corpse's ankle.

"No...no...," Vinny didn't want to get closer, but Vance nudged him.

Vinny's hangdog expression perplexed Corba until Vance explained.

"I think my brother was sweet on Evita."

Corba nodded.

"We all were, son," Corba said solemnly, and Vinny wondered if Evita sucked off the creepy doctor too. *Of course she did, you stupid cuck! She blew everyone on the Arkham payroll!* Vinny imagined William Sr.'s ancient, leathery dick crammed in Evita's mouth and shuddered...two parts disgust, one part sexual titillation.

"Evita died for the cause. She *sacrificed* herself for the cause," Corba said. "She will be remembered as a hero for what she did tonight."

"What are those...names?" Vinny tried to make sense of the letters etched into Evita's flesh—Dagon, Yog-Sothoth, Azathoth, Nyogtha.

"The Deacons' bosses," Vance whispered and Vinny nodded. *If you think we're assholes, you should meet her!*

"Help me unload these tools," Corba said. He bent over as far as his belly would allow and pulled a pink-stained rib spreader from beneath the stretcher. He handed it to Vance.

"Put this in the van," Corba said. He handed Vinny a bone saw with a discolored blade. "Give this to your brother. He knows where it goes."

Vinny groaned. The corpse's chest gaped open, insides scooped out, breasts, once beautiful, hanging flat and lifeless at odd angles.

Strange Creations' bass player Bobby Marks stormed around the back of Allen's bus. He pulled on the front door. Locked. He stomped over and Corba hastily covered the corpse with the sheet. Vance helped him load the stretcher into the back of the van.

"Is Evita in there?" Bobby asked.

"Listen, Bobby…it was our understanding Evita wasn't your girl anymore," Vance said

Vinny set the bone saw down in the back of the van and Corba slammed the doors closed. The doctor looked ready to piss his pants.

"Allen Vent is a murdering maniac!" Bobby screamed. He looked ready to cry. "He won't get away with this and neither will you!"

Corba jumped in the van and took off, his door slamming closed as the vehicle peeled out, showering Vinny, Vance, and Bobby with dust.

"Bobby…maybe you should talk to Howard Phillips," Vance said, watching Corba's taillights fade.

"Fuck him, too!" Bobby said. He stormed off toward Allen's bus, climbing the rear ladder onto the vehicle's roof.

"What's his problem?" Vinny asked.

"He's an asshole," Vance said, watching Bobby drop

down into Allen's bus through the skylight. "Let's go."

They almost made it back to their bus when Howard ran up with Donald, Allen's bus driver. Howard ran, *ran*, which Vinny took as a sure sign of the impending apocalypse.

"Vin! Van! Have you seen Bobby or Allen?" Howard said.

Vance jerked his thumb toward Allen's bus.

"What's wrong?"

"Ritchie overdosed," Howard said, looking back toward Ritchie's bus, his face a mask of worry. "The paramedics are with him, but it doesn't look good. We have to get out of here."

"Fuck," Vance said. A medical vehicle was parked next to Ritchie's bus, lights flashing. A second ambulance pulled up while Vance and Vinny watched.

Vinny once wished Ritchie Smith dead, but now that it was finally happening, he didn't care much either way. There was no escaping Arkham and, without Evita, nothing else mattered.

"Looks like you got your wish, bro," Vance said. Vinny hated when his brother read his mind, though he was used to it. "Ritchie's checking out."

"Doesn't matter," Vinny sighed. Paramedics carried a stretcher off Ritchie's bus, put it into the back of an ambulance, and sped away. "The Deacons are shipping us off to study with Smoke Johnson."

"What?" Vance asked. "Who?"

Howard and Donald briefly reappeared, Howard barking orders, before running off again. *Howard Phillips is running. We're all doomed.*

"Smoke Johnson is an old blues guy who taught the Strange Creations 'The Summoning Song,'" Vinny explained. "He's supposed to show us the 'right' way to play the song in case we need to fill in for Ritchie."

"Fuck that!" Vance said. "We *already* know how to play the song. I'm getting my feel for the music back. Did you hear my ass-kicking yodel tonight? Howard should let us try again."

Maybe not all of Vance's addictions were cured. Vinny shook his head as they walked toward the bus.

"Arkham wants Allen Vent to play it," Vinny said. "We're strictly sidemen."

"Come on! Thom is a ten-times-better drummer than Mick the fucking Stick!" Vance said.

"Ten times bigger too," Vinny said.

"At least," Vance replied. "Why doesn't Arkham get Smoked Salmon to fill in for Ritchie?"

"Guy's really old," Vinny shrugged. "He has mobility issues according to Howard."

"Christ, another gimp!" Vance said. "Does Arkham get tax credits for hiring the fucking disabled!"

"Hey, they didn't discriminate against your mental illness…or Pegdick's deadness," Vinny said.

"I'm not mentally ill anymore," Vance said, his jaw set.

"What are you now, Vance?" Vinny asked, afraid of the answer. "Are you a true believer in The Great Work like Thom…and…and… Did you drink the Arkham Kool Aid too?"

Vance shook his head.

"I only drink water so my tissues don't dry out," Vance said. "Smoking really dehydrates you."

"Do you believe in what we're doing, Vance?"

"Does anyone *believe* in what they're doing, Vinny, or do you put your helmet on and do it?" Vance asked. "You have a job to do, you do it."

Their bus idled outside the stadium and departed immediately after they boarded, leaving a wake of dust in the San Antonio night. Several hours later, Vinny awoke to his brother shouting from the back of the bus.

"Smoke Johnson is, like, the gayest name *ever*!"

CHAPTER SIXTEEN
Burning For You

When you boarded the Arkham jet, you never knew where or when you'd land. There were no tickets, no checked luggage, no itinerary. The Boyle brothers took off from a small airfield near Fort Stockton, Texas, but Vinny had no idea of their destination.

The buses drove thirty-six hours straight. The rest of the crew turned north at Sheffield, TX, but Vance and Vinny's bus pressed on west along I-10. Vinny's heart sank watching the other buses take a different fork in the road, their caravan disappearing into the night.

"Is the tour still on?" Vance asked. Their driver didn't answer. His name was Pauleo and he'd lost his tongue during a merchandising dispute in Nuevo Leon several years back.

Vinny called and texted, but Howard took several hours to respond.

"There's a plane waiting for you in Fort Stockton," Howard said, sounding tinny and small through the speaker phone. "I'll see you when you land and introduce you to Smoke."

Ritchie Smith died...for four minutes. Paramedics

revived him and Arkham shipped him off to rehab. The tour would resume in South America next month.

"This is the perfect opportunity to woodshed with Mr. Johnson and get a feel for what Arkham needs," Howard said.

They flew for nearly five hours and landed someplace cold and gray, the clouds so low and dark, Vinny needed to check his phone for the day and time. It was Thursday afternoon, just after three. The airport consisted of a long runway, a small shed, and an enormous airplane hangar. Vinny and Vance descended a metal staircase to the tarmac, as Howard and Donald stepped out of a black Towne Car.

"Greetings, gentlemen," Howard said. His shark-tooth smile and sharp suit were back, which brought Vinny an uneasy comfort.

"Where are we?" Vinny asked.

Howard looked surprised.

"At music lessons!" Howard said. "Come inside and meet Master Smoke! This weather is for shit."

They followed Howard and Donald into the airplane hangar. Vance nudged Vinny, showing him the GPS on his phone. They were in a town Vinny'd never heard of in northwest New Jersey, called Franz Rock.

Vinny expected to find crew members inside the hangar, but there was only vast, black emptiness. One corner of the hangar was illuminated and furnished, though it looked hastily arranged. The space revolved around three upright pianos with benches, two ratty futons, and a few stringed instruments. (Vinny's Les Paul and six-string bass were there, along with Vance's violin.) A big, wooden packing crate sat in the center of it all.

"What the hell is this?" Vinny asked.

"Your home for the next few weeks," Howard said.

"Make yourselves comfortable."

He and Donald slipped off their jackets. Donald held a crowbar in his fist.

"What the fuck?" Vance said. He planted his feet and assumed a fighting stance. Vinny balanced on his toes, prepared to run.

"Calm down, boys," Howard said. "We mean you no harm."

Howard nodded and Donald used the crowbar to pry nails from the top of the wooden crate.

"We're not staying here for three weeks," Vance said.

"This kind of intensive training will transform your musical lives, gentlemen. One-on-one—well, one-on-two, in this case—private tutoring with a true musical master," Howard said.

"Where is Smoke Johnson?" Vinny asked.

"Arkham feels a secluded environment is most beneficial to learning," Howard said, helping Donald with the lid. "No distractions."

"Come on, Howard," Vance said. "We can't live in an empty airplane hangar for three weeks."

"Sure you can! Everything you need is here. A kitchen…showers…" Howard's idea of a facilities tour was pointing into the darkness. "You'll find the wifi password on a piece of paper taped to the front of the fridge."

It sounds like a summer rental. "Do you get a lot of clients with private planes vacationing in Bumblefuck, New Jersey?" Vinny asked.

"Not really." Howard answered without listening. Donald pulled the final nail from the lid.

"Where's Smoke Johnson?" Vinny asked again. Howard's smile made Vinny's stomach drop.

"Right here, Vin!" Howard said. "Gentlemen, meet your

new music teacher, the illustrious Smoke Johnson!"

Howard and Donald lifted the lid off the crate and the smell of burnt pork hit Vinny like a slap in the face. *Is Evita in there?* Hope leapt in Vinny's chest, but what rose from the crate wasn't Evita. Vinny wasn't sure it was even human. Fire damage turned its flesh to mottled, black char, erasing all distinguishing features, even gender. Smoke drifted from pitted craters in the creature's skin and it stood with the pop and snap of stiff bones, the crackle of burnt flesh.

Vinny screamed and Vance cursed.

Smoke Johnson opened his eyes. The orbs, shot through with dark, red veins, bulged from his withered, flamed-dried skull. He smiled and his scorched lips tore like paper, revealing a flash of awful yellow teeth. Smoke waved. This time Vance screamed and Vinny cursed.

"It's the Burning Bum!" Vance cried.

"Who?" Vinny asked.

"The Burning Bum! One of The Strange Creations' stage props," Vance said. "It pops up at the end of every show. Haven't you seen it before?"

"No," Vinny said. The smoking creature lowered its hand while Howard and Donald dismantled the rest of the packing crate. Smoke kept smiling though his shredded lips.

"You never watched the band we open up for?"

"No," Vinny repeated. "Who's the Burning Bum?"

"It's a smoldering body that pops out of a box during 'Midnight Tour,'" Vance said. "I thought it was fake."

"The Burning Bum *is* fake. This is the *real* Smoke Johnson," Howard said. "You really should have watched Allen Vent perform once or twice, Vinny. Shame on you."

"So the Burning Bum is based on...*him*?" Vance pointed to Smoke. "That's pretty insensitive, Howard, no?"

Howard shrugged.

"Allen Vent and The Strange Creations can be real assholes," Howard explained.

"We noticed," Vinny said.

"Why is he still smoking?" Vance asked. "Can't you put him out?"

"Honestly? No. We've tried," Howard explained. "We're not sure why Smoke smokes. He may be experiencing some kind of eternal punishment for past deeds. Smoke's soul is burning, from the inside out, and soulfire can only be extinguished by God himself…or, Raylat Mnoogth, Lord Of Human Entrails. Hopefully we'll run into Ray once the Infinitus opens. Then Smoke can finally quit smoking. It's bad for your health, Smoke!"

Howard smiled at the smoldering monster. The monster extended its middle finger to Howard, tossed its head back, and made a sound like two lions fighting, half primal roar, half death scream. Its awful laugh made Vinny cringe.

Howard slipped his jacket back on, while Donald cleared away the packing crate. The smoking creature walked to the piano in the middle, pulled out the bench with its foot, and sat down.

"Go ahead, boys," Howard said. "Donald and I will leave you three to work."

"You're not leaving us alone here with…*him*!" Vinny pointed at Smoke's back.

"Grow up, Vincent," Howard said. "You're in no danger. You can leave the lights on if you're afraid of the dark."

"How are we gonna stay here? What about our shit?" Vance said. "Cigarettes? Weed?"

"You have a one-track mind, Vance," Howard scowled. "But you'll find the kitchen and bathroom medicine cabinet well-stocked with everything you require. Arkham provides."

"What about our clothes?" Vinny asked.

"Your bus arrives from Texas the day after tomorrow," Howard said. "I'm sure you boys can rough it for a couple of days. There are clean sweatpants and Arkham T-shirts in the storage closet."

"Where's that?" Vance asked. Howard pointed to a random spot in the dark.

"You can't leave us here, Howard," Vinny repeated, hating how whiny he sounded. He couldn't help it. "We don't even know what's going on. Is Ritchie okay? Are we still the opening act?"

"Ritchie Smith is in drug treatment until the end of the month. As you know, the recidivism rate is very high for drug abusers, so either or both of you may be called to fill in when the tour resumes, which is why you're here to learn the parts," Howard sighed. "Don't stall for time by asking questions you already know the answers to, Vinny, and don't worry about things you needn't worry about. Concern yourself with playing the song correctly. You'll be fine."

He and Donald departed before Vinny could ask more questions, leaving the Boyle brothers alone with Smoke Johnson.

The creature beckoned them with a smoking fingertip. Vance approached the piano. Smoke made a peace sign, closed it, and put his charred fingers to his torn lips. Vance lit a cigarette and handed it to him. Smoke clenched the butt between his yellow teeth, and began to play, blackened fingers smudging the white keys.

He played a piece by Franz Liszt, melding into Rachmaninoff, followed by Mozart, Chopin, and Schubert. Smoke played on and on, fingers gliding over the keys, charred feet working the pedals.

Vance and Vinny sat at the pianos on either side, watching him play. Smoke broke into a ragtime boogie and Vance joined him on the second verse, Vinny coming in two measures later. They played in unison for two verses and then Smoke played a strange harmony to their melody. Vance caught up with him, but Smoke switched it up again, playing a contra-punctual part that boggled Vinny's mind, left him flailing around the keyboard. Vance really improved on keys, sounding like his old self, while Vinny's fingers felt like bloated sausage links. Too much time on guitar made his keyboard skills rusty.

They played for hours, pausing only to light cigarettes. Finally, Vinny held up his hands and stood.

"I need a break," he said.

"Me too." Vance stood. "Smoke?"

Smoke pointed to the empty cigarette pack atop his piano and went back to playing a soft, disjointed melody. Smoke didn't take breaks.

"Cool. I'll get a fresh pack," Vance said.

They used their phone flashlights to find the bathroom. The cabinets were stocked—heat wraps, aspirin, benedryl, marijuana, Xanax. Vance found a volcano-style marijuana vaporizer and spare balloons in the back of a closet. They took the vaporizer, pot, and Xanax into the kitchen. The fridge contained fresh meat and produce, the cabinets a plethora of pre-packaged foods, along with ten cartons of Marlboros. The Boyles grabbed two cold beers each, a carton of cigarettes, and a box of Twinkies, before returning to the rehearsal space.

Smoke kept playing, but the Boyles didn't join him. They sprawled on the futons, Vinny tearing into the Twinkies, Vance firing up the vaporizer. Vinny didn't realize how tired he was until he sat down, and, after two balloons of pure THC, the feeling amplified. He sipped his beer and closed his eyes.

"Smoke, play us some Delta blues," Vance said. Smoke flashed the peace sign and Vance got him a fresh cigarette. Smoke lit it with the tip of his finger and launched into a blues mash-up featuring Little Willie Littlefield, Pinetop Smith, and Barrelhouse Chuck.

"How about some old-school Bach?" Vinny asked.

Smoke switched on a dime, turning loose, boogie-woogie blues into staid Baroque passages.

"Awesome," Vance said, fitting a fresh balloon onto the vaporizer. "It's like having a living jukebox! Well, not exactly living."

Smoke flipped Vance the bird over his shoulder, charred middle finger trailing fumes, but never missed a note of the Goldberg Variations.

CHAPTER SEVENTEEN
Across the Universe

They ate psychedelic mushrooms for breakfast and spent the next day playing Beatles songs in three-part harmony, giggling as visible notes drifted from Smoke's piano, shapes and colors overlapping in mid-air. Vance ditched the vaporizer in favor of rolling cigar-like joints. He passed one to Smoke, who sucked half of it down in one toke. Smoke laughed when he exhaled and it sounded like high-speed trains colliding. They smoked, ate junk food, and played more Beatles, this time with Vinny on viola and Vance on violin. They napped, woke, and did it again, Vinny on guitar, Vance switching between saxophone and oboe.

Late on the second night, the Boyles curled on their futons, nearly asleep, Smoke Johnson played a song with an amazing opening run. The air swirled with spirits and the Boyle brothers rose from their stupor, watching Smoke's skeletal fingers work the piano like they were watching a fireworks display—oohing and ahhing, occasionally covering their ears in terror. They sat at their pianos, but didn't play until Smoke's third time through. They joined in and didn't stop until noon the following day. They napped, woke, and did it again.

Their bus arrived that afternoon, Howard Phillips following in the Towne Car. Pauleo parked the vehicle inside the hangar and Donald handed bags of fast food to the Boyle brothers.

"I'm looking forward to sleeping in my own bed," Vance said around a mouthful of burger. "Futon is fucking killing me."

"You're already dead!" Vinny pointed at his brother.

"Touché."

"The bus is at your disposal," Howard said. "At the end of the month, the bus will take you to JFK Airport, where you will board a flight to Caracas, Venezuela. There, you will board a bus remarkably similar to this one, which will take you to your next gig."

"How's Ritchie Smith?" Vinny asked.

"He's alive and in drug rehab. That's all I really know," Howard said. "But there's another drama brewing within The Strange Creations."

"That band is a fucking soap opera," Vance said.

"Indeed, rarely have I ever encountered a bigger bunch of drama queens," Howard said. "But Arkham has a plan which will resolve the band's infighting as well as hasten the opening of the Infinitus. Come."

They followed Howard onto the bus.

"We're losing Bobby Marks," Howard said once they were seated.

"Good," Vance said. "Guy's an asshole."

"Have you seen Evita?" Vinny asked.

Howard and Vance both looked at Vinny as if he'd passed gas.

"I mean, could you bring her back, the way you did with Smoke?"

"Christ, Vin!" Vance exclaimed. "You *saw* her!"

Howard held up a hand.

"Why should we bring Evita back, Vinny?" Howard said.

Vinny looked from Howard to his brother, blushing deep red.

"I don't know...I thought, maybe...you could bring her back..."

"Vinny, there's no reason to do that," Howard explained slowly. "Evita gave her best to our effort and she did not die in vain. She helped us tremendously and we all miss her. But we have to move on. Okay, Vinny?"

Vinny looked down and nodded.

"Is Bobby quitting the band?" he asked, eager to change the subject. "I *know* I can play *his* parts."

"Not exactly," Howard said. "Bobby Marks plays a bigger role in this than bass guitar. He brings the one vital ingredient needed to open the Infinitus. Love."

The word hung in the air until Vance shot it down.

"That's...so...gay!" he shouted.

"I don't know if you're expressing merriment or homophobia, Van, but neither has any bearing on Bobby's role in our organization," Howard said. "Bobby has a wife and child whom he adores, yet purposely keeps away from the tour. Arkham needs that love-bond to open the Infinitus, but Bobby withholds this valuable resource from us. All of us. You...me...the whole Arkham organization."

"Who would marry that asshole?" Vance asked. "Let alone breed with him? Girls are stupid."

"The one who married Bobby is, and I'm sure she regrets it now," Howard said. "Bobby and his wife haven't seen each other for nearly five years, but they're still very much in love. They worship their daughter and parent-child love is the strongest bond of all. Well, in most cases,"

A quick flash of Pegdick's Biggest Drug Fuck-Ups

flickered through Vinny's mind.

"All you need is love?" he asked. "To open the Infinitus?"

"Love is all you need," Howard smiled, wide and sharky. "Well, exceptional musical talent, too...and blood sacrifices, of course...and a base of disciples of a certain size and caliber. But yes, love is the most important part of the equation...at least it's the part giving us the most difficulty."

"Why?"

"True love...pure love, is hard to find, Vinny," Howard explained. "Neither Allen nor the rest of The Strange Creations had much to offer. Thom Thomas has a strained relationship with his parents and brother. And the two of you...well, why do you think you're still here, together, after...all that's occurred?"

Howard rested two fingertips against his temple and glanced at Vance.

"Subtle, Howard," Vance said.

"Regardless, Vincent's love is what's keeping you going right now, Vance," Howard said. "Reanimation doesn't work unless someone *really* wants you to come back."

Vance smiled on his brother.

"Thanks, bro!" Vance said.

"Cool," Vinny replied. "Did I...did I keep Pegdick going too?"

"Yes," Howard replied.

"You're a good son, Vinny," Vance said. "And a great brother."

"Brotherly love is a powerful bond and probably the reason Arkham hired you," Howard said. "But those bonds are already tapped, given the circumstances, and, even so, pale in comparison to what Bobby brings to the table...or won't, as the case may be."

"So what's Arkham's big plan?" Vance asked. "Kidnap Bobby's wife and kid?"

"When you put it in those terms, Vance, it sounds quite vulgar."

Vinny jumped to his feet, rattling the ashtray on the table.

"No way," he said. "We're not kidnapping anyone. Especially not a child!"

"Sit down, Vinny! By golly, you are a cesspool of bubbling emotion!" Howard intoned, but Vinny didn't sit until his brother said. "We're not kidnapping anyone, Vin. It's cool, bro."

"Indeed, no one is getting kidnapped. Bobby's wife and daughter will join the tour willingly," Howard said. "Once here, however, there are concerns Bobby may either drive them away again, or flee with them, at which point you may be called upon to help persuade the Marks family to stay until the end of the show."

"We're not hurting anyone, Howard." Vinny shook his head. "The clean-up work for Allen…that's one thing. It's fucked up, but it's one thing. But we're not holding people hostage and we're not hurting children."

"'Kidnapping! Hostage!' Such grossly exaggerated terms, Vin!" Howard said. "All Arkham wants is your help *persuading* the Marks family to stay in the *unlikely* event they decide to leave, okay?"

"Listen, Howard," Vance said. "My brother and I aren't cut out for muscle work. Get real here. Can't you find anyone better suited for this job?"

Howard nodded.

"Satan's Riders Motorcycle Club will handle all of our security needs on the South American leg. They are our first and second line of defense should a situation occur," Howard said. "You guys are third string. The likelihood of you ever seeing action is very low."

"We're not hurting anyone," Vinny said, crossing his arms and tucking his chin to his chest.

"No problem, Vinny," Howard said, glancing at Vance. "We're not asking you to do that. I'm simply trying to prepare you gentlemen for what may lie ahead. 'By failing to prepare, you are preparing to fail.' Wise words from Benjamin Franklin."

"He was a fat douche," Vance said. "Speaking of which, what's Thom up to?"

"Mr. Thomas checked into an excellent rehabilitation facility for weight management and control of his diabetes," Howard said. "He's going to lose his killer kick drum foot if he doesn't stop eating chocolate."

"Can't you put a magic bean in his foot and make him keep going?" Vinny asked.

"Magic bean. That's funny, Vin," Howard said. "Glad to have you back."

"You should get Thom gastric bypass surgery," Vance said. "Dude's gonna die."

"When we get him down under five hundred pounds, the doctors will do exactly that," Howard explained. "But Thom needs to meet us halfway."

"Not without a forklift," Vinny said. Vance snickered.

"Brilliant, Vin. Your talent as a comedian is dwarfed only by your poor taste in women," Howard said. Vinny fell silent and pouty. Vance shot Howard an angry look.

"Sorry. I shouldn't have said that," Howard said. "I'm not as clever or funny as you boys. But nothing is gained by fat-shaming Thom. He's doing the best he can. We all are."

Vance nodded out the bus window, where Smoke sat motionless at the piano.

"Is Smoke still around because somebody loves him?"

Vance asked. The question got Vinny's attention.

"It wouldn't surprise me if there are great loves pining away for Smoke Johnson," Howard said. "He's a musician. Women find those types sexy, in case you haven't noticed. But hate is an equally powerful motivator and Smoke racked up many enemies. Judging from his ever-smoldering state, it appears he's suffering an eternal, Greek-style punishment."

"He's an excellent piano player," Vinny said. "Let him play with Allen Vent and open your...whatever..."

Howard looked exasperated.

"Vinny, Vinny...so contrary. I agree, Smoke is an exceptionally talented pianist and, while your suggestion is appreciated, it doesn't fit Arkham's plan, and therefore is not constructive," Howard said. "Does Smoke look like he's ready to hit the road?"

"Audiences would love it if the Burning Bum came to life and started jamming, even if it's a one-time thing," Vance said. "I still think the Burning Bum is insensitive. I'm surprised the Society To Prevent Homelessness isn't on your ass for encouraging fans to set fire to transients."

"Not *my* fans, Vance. Allen Vent fans. Strange Creations fans," Howard said. "And don't give anybody any ideas. We've got enough problems on this tour already."

"You could tell people Smoke is animatronic...or a hologram, like Tupac," Vinny suggested.

"That could work," Vance nodded. "You gotta hand it to my brother...smart, funny, *and* handsome!"

"Your brother looks for excuses to avoid what is asked of him," Howard said. "I will take your suggestions under advisement, Vinny, but I urge the two of you to spend the rest of your time here preparing yourself for the upcoming tour, which includes following the plans discussed today. Is that understood?"

"Yes, mother." Vinny coughed into his fist. "*Fucker*!"

"Very mature, Vincent." Howard coughed into his fist. "*Douche*! Please, boys. Take Old Ben's advice. 'An ounce of prevention is worth a pound of cure.' Be ready."

"Stop quoting obese, flatulent, bags of shit," Vance said. "And give Thom our best when you see him."

"He's hard to miss," Vinny added.

Howard left the bus.

Vinny expected Vance to recap Howard's visit, discuss Bobby Marks…Evita…life and death…anything. But Vance stared out the bus window and smoked instead. Vinny lit up too. Howard piled into the Towne Car with Donald and Pauleo and they pulled out, the garage door closing automatically behind them. Vinny and Vance were sealed back inside the hangar with Smoke, who smoldered on the piano bench, a Halloween decoration, a funhouse horror.

"We should eat the rest of those mushrooms and toke," Vance said, snubbing out his cigarette. "Then jam."

Good. Vinny needed a simple, tangible plan. Making music with Vance always comforted him, even if the song demanded sacrifice and sucked away your soul.

They returned to their pianos and began to play. Smoke's jaw opened wide, scorched throat emitting a terrible, car-crash laugh. The song went on for twenty-eight days. Smoke and Vance could go non-stop as long as they had cigarettes and weed, but Vinny made his brother take breaks. Vinny still needed to eat and use the bathroom, but found cocaine and Ecstasy in the medicine cabinet and didn't sleep for nearly a week. When he did, he dreamed of a beautiful burnt woman with Smoke's heinous laugh, who forced his hands deep inside her hollowed-out chest cavity until he screamed.

CHAPTER EIGHTEEN
Tonight's The Night

Allen Vent and The Strange Creations played ten shows in South America, the last in Rio De Janeiro. The last two stops on the tour, in Argentina, were cancelled when the world ended.

Nothing changed with Allen Vent and The Strange Creations, except Bobby Marks got a bad haircut (which Vance dubbed, "Totally! Fucking! Gay!"), and Ritchie got hooked on drugs again as soon as the tour resumed. Thom Thomas remained fat and cranky, displeased with his new dietary restrictions, constantly asking Vinny and Vance (or anyone else) to buy him chocolate bars whenever they approached a vending machine.

The equatorial heat messed with Vinny's head in Caracas, made him woozy, verging on fever-induced hallucinations. Black holes appeared in the sky after Allen Vent and The Strange Creations' second night in Venezuela and Vinny asked his brother if he saw them too.

"Oh, they are most definitely there, bro," Vance said. "Everybody sees them. Haven't you watched the news?"

"Of course not," Vinny said. "It's fake bullshit."

"Well, the holes in the sky aren't bullshit," Vance said.

"Scientists are baffled. Three probes have gone up in as many days. They have theories, but they really don't know shit."

"It's the song," Vinny said, more statement than question.

"It demands sacrifice," Vance said. "I guess it got what it wanted and now it's ready to give birth."

The song came around again a week later in Peru. Vinny watched the entire Strange Creations' show from backstage. He felt a twinge of jealously watching the crowd react to Allen Vent's every move, screaming with ecstasy every time Ritchie Smith tore into a guitar solo. He and Vance needed to work on their stage presence.

The final song showcased the Burning Bum. A dancing hobo puppet dressed in rags sprung from a box in the middle of the stage and burst into flames. The fans went wild and many came prepared, tossing paper and trash into the flames, feeding it to a frenzy. Vinny understood his brother's outrage. Howard said Smoke Johnson was the driving force behind The Strange Creations, a founding member, and this was how the band repaid him, by burning him in effigy night after night? What dicks.

Once you got past Smoke's charred pork odor, communication challenges, and terrifying appearance, he was a good guy and an excellent musician. Vinny reluctantly said good-bye to Smoke when their month in New Jersey ended. As much as he wanted to flee the vast claustrophobic emptiness of the airplane hangar, the idea of going back on tour, especially an Evita-less tour, filled him with trepidation. What was the point?

"We gotta bring Smoke's song into the world, Vin. The Strange Creations forgot what he taught them," Vance explained. Smoke gave them each a fist bump that scorched their knuckles before they boarded the bus to

JFK.

But The Strange Creations hadn't forgotten their maestro's magic. Ritchie and Allen started the song together, their playing so intimate, so pure, it gave Vinny goosebumps. Inky, black clouds blossomed out of thin air, raining down strange, bestial shapes, while fingers of mist steamed from the ground and snaked around the legs of the audience members. Fans dropped and twisted themselves into the same pretzel-like poses Vinny's parents once assumed (*Satanic yoga!*). Cracks split the sky and long squid arms rose from the crowd, beautiful and terrifying, waving screaming teenagers around.

They played San Paulo on Thursday. The Horrors' entire opening act was one, feedback-laden, thirty-five minute song Vance called "Permutations In The Key Of Madness." It earned a solid chorus of boos from the audience. Allen Vent and The Strange Creations closed with a forty-five minute "Whipping Post" that left everyone, audience and band alike, emotionally drained. Ritchie Smith played like a god.

The Saturday show in Rio De Janeiro was a live HBO broadcast. Everybody backstage at Maracana Stadium was jumpy, which Vinny didn't fully understand until he spoke with Howard.

"We have word Bobby's wife and daughter have arrived and are making their way to the stadium," Howard told him. "Tonight's the night, Vinny. Ready?"

"I'm not hurting anyone," Vinny said.

"A simple 'yes' will do, Vin," Howard replied. "Six-Pack and Pike from Satan's Riders will look after Patricia and Peppermint once they arrive. You needn't worry about a thing."

"Bobby's daughter is named Peppermint?" Vance asked. "That's…adorable."

"Peppermint Patty Marks is her full name," Howard said. "I was there the day she was born. She truly is adorable."

Vinny's flesh crawled. Howard *knew* this kid, yet still wanted to sacrifice her and her mother? Vinny told Howard again he wouldn't harm anyone.

"Will you stop saying that! Nobody is asking you to harm anyone, Vin!" Howard said. "Just back up Six-Pack and Pike if they need it, okay? Okay!"

Howard left Vinny and Vance backstage two hours before showtime.

"Let's get high," Vance suggested. They walked toward their bus, but girlish squeals distracted them. A little girl, Vinny guessed around six years old, ran toward the stage, dragging a woman by the hand. A minute later Bobby Marks leapt off stage and ran to embrace his family, like a scene from a Hallmark movie. Vinny's throat tightened and his eyes welled up.

There's the real power, right there, Vinny thought, watching Bobby hold his wife and daughter. *If only Evita...* Vinny shook his head like a dog to stop the thought from coming.

"Meet tonight's blood sacrifice," Vance said, nodding toward Bobby's family as he lit a cigarette. "Mommy's got a nice ass."

Vinny slapped the cigarette out of his brother's mouth.

"Fuck's your problem? You've had a bug up your ass since we got to South America," Vance said. "When will you realize we're doing a job here, and yes, it's not the job we were hired for, but it's the job we have. Our roles are important, Vinny! The Boyle brothers are changing the world! People will remember us! Why are you such a mope?"

"I don't want to be remembered as the brothers who

ended the world!" Vinny said.

"Why not?" Vance asked. "The world is a piece of shit, Vinny. It's been that way ever since human beings started crawling around the surface. Things aren't getting better, in case you haven't noticed. We're in a downward spiral, like a flushing toilet. It's time to hit the reset button!"

"No, it is not!" Vinny shouted. "You were the same way in grade school! Whenever you couldn't solve a problem in front of the class, you'd attack the smartboard until you got sent to the principal's office. Why don't you try to *solve* problems instead of blowing everything up? Why don't you *fix* things instead of destroying them?"

"The world's too far gone, Vin," Vance said. "And so are we."

"I'm not," Vinny said, glancing toward Bobby's family. "I'm helping them get out of here tonight. Don't try to stop me."

"Christ, Vin! You and your white knight bullshit!" Vance said. "You pulled the same shit with that whore! You think you can save everybody! Here comes Super Vinny to the rescue!"

"I'm not a superhero, asshole, I'm just trying to be a normal human being!" Vinny said. "Christ, Vance, Howard never should have brought you back. I wish he had let you go when you shot yourself in Panama City."

"Sure, and Pegdick should have smothered me in the crib and let you live," Vance said. "You could be normal if you didn't have to take care of your crazy twin brother. But that's not the way it worked out. We're here. Now. And we have a job to do. Stop living in what-ifs and coulda-beens. Live in the moment. That's all we have, Vin."

Before Vinny could answer, commotion erupted around Bobby Marks and his family. His wife was screaming, and the little girl looked scared. So did Howard Phillips. A gray

Towne Car rolled through the cargo bay door and parked next to Howard. Pike and Six-Pack got out.

"Shit," Vinny said. The little girl cowered behind her mother's leg.

More yelling, followed by pushing and shoving. Pike opened the rear door, while Six-Pack shoved the mother and daughter into the back of the car. Bobby shouted, and Howard tried calming him. Six-Pack slammed the door and the Towne Car sped away through the cargo doors.

"See? Problem solved," Vance said. "Out of sight, out of mind. Bye-bye, phat-assed Mommy!"

"No, Vance. Not 'out of mind,'" Vinny said. "Where do you think they're going? To a suite at the Hilton?"

"Don't know, don't care," Vance said. "Time to get high."

"I'm going to find them." Vince walked off toward the cargo bay.

"Why do you give a shit?" his brother asked.

"Because you're supposed to," Vinny called back.

"You're an asshole," Vance shouted.

"You're a monster," Vinny replied.

Vinny passed by Howard and Bobby. He intended to tell Howard exactly what he planned to do. This madness had to end. But Bobby punched Howard in the face and Howard crumpled to the ground. Bobby looked like he wanted to kick him, but thought better of it. He stalked off to his trailer, slamming the door behind him. Nobody stopped him. Six-Pack knelt next to Howard and a few crew members trotted over. Vinny broke into a run too and arrived as Pike and Six-Pack hauled Howard to his feet. Howard pulled his hand away from his face and his jaw fell open, swinging freely. Two teeth floated in a pool of blood in his palm.

"Fit. *Fit*!" Howard attempted to curse. Six-Pack held

Howard up, but Howard threw his arms around Vinny's neck.

"Inny!" Howard said. "Oh-yea!"

"What?""

"Ore-va!" Howard was emphatic, holding his jaw closed with his hand, pleading with his eyes.

"I don't understand," Vinny said.

"He wants you to take him to Dr. Corba," Pike interpreted.

Howard nodded, blood dribbling down his chin. He mimed instructions to Six-Pack and Pike and the pair trotted off toward the cargo bay. Vinny stumble-dragged Howard to Corba's trailer in the far corner of the arena.

"What are you planning to do with Bobby's family?" Vinny asked.

Howard shook his head.

"I'm going to find them and let them go," Vinny said. "This blood sacrifice shit ends tonight. It should have ended long ago."

Howard couldn't say anything, but shot Vinny a wide-eyed look of disapproval.

"Arkham's plan is shit, Howard," Vinny said. "*You're* shit. You used me and my brother, you manipulated me *through* my brother and vice versa. You turned us into killers. You ruined our lives! My parents... You killed my entire family and now you want to do the same to Bobby Marks...to that poor, little girl!"

Howard leaned on Vinny shoulder and rubbed his fingers together beside his head. Vinny thought he was asking for money until he realized Howard was playing the world's smallest violin. Vinny tried to drop Howard on his ass, but they'd reached Dr. Corba's trailer and Howard lunged against the door, banging on it. It took a while for Corba to answer. He looked sleepy.

"Oh, dear!" Corba said when he saw Howard's face. "Come inside! You too, Vinny. I'll need help."

Howard grabbed Vinny's wrist and pulled him inside. Howard flopped on a kitchen chair and Corba cleaned his mouth with gauze. Corba asked Vinny to pour a glass of milk and when Vinny set it down, Corba tossed Howard's loose teeth into the liquid. ("We'll see what we can do with those later.") Corba tried to give Howard pills, but Howard pointed to his throat and shook his head. He couldn't swallow. Corba nodded and returned the pills to his medical bag. He pulled out a tub of the minty blue gel they'd used to soothe their severed toes. Corba slathered strips of gauze with magic balm and stuffed them inside Howard's mouth until his right cheek puffed out like a chipmunk.

Someone banged on the trailer door.

"Dr. Corba?" Vance's voice came from outside. "Have you seen Howard or my brother?"

Corba let Vance in and Vinny filled him in.

"I told you Bobby Marks was an asshole," Vance told Howard.

Howard nodded. Dr. Corba wrapped his jaw shut.

"We're due on stage in ten minutes," Vance told Vinny. "Time is tight because of the live broadcast. Everybody's looking for you. Thom's freaking out. His head is about to explode."

Howard shooed the brothers toward the door. They stood still. Howard pointed to his wrist, which was devoid of a watch, and pointed toward the door. They still didn't move, so Howard kicked them in the seat of the pants until the Boyles left the trailer.

"That was fun," Vance said, heading toward the stage.

"Yeah," Vinny replied.

They opened the set with "Collie Flower" and rolled

hard into "Curmudgeon." Vance hopped behind the piano and teased a bit of "The Summoning Song," Vinny accompanying him on viola, until Thom broke it up with a big beat that became "Bad Moon Rising." They closed with "Lucille Sounds Funny Tonight," Thom's drums shaking earth and sky, Vance's yodel so sweet and pure, it brought Vinny to tears.

Vinny bid the audience good night, surprised to hear a good round of applause. Allen waited in the wings, holding up Bobby Marks. Bobby wore mirrored sunglasses and looked dead on his feet. *What kind of drugs is he on?*

"Are you okay, Bobby?" Vinny asked.

"He's fine," Allen answered.

"Do you need me to sit in for him?" Vinny asked.

"Fuck...off," Bobby said.

"Okay, have a great show," Vinny said, muttering under his breath, "Asshole."

Allen held up a finger, making Vinny wait. He handed Bobby off to a roadie who helped Bobby strap on his bass. Allen nodded at Vinny and pointed up. Vinny didn't catch on. Allen looked up. So did Vinny. People moved on the catwalk above the stage, a pretty woman and young girl among them.

"Go," Allen Vent said.

Vinny set his jaw.

"No," he said.

Allen cocked his head like a confused animal.

"Your brother's up there," Allen said.

Vinny dropped his bass and ran across the stage to the stairs leading up to the catwalk. The stage lights dimmed and the capacity crowd at Maracana Stadium roared as one, welcoming Allen Vent and The Strange Creations to the greatest show on earth.

CHAPTER NINETEEN

When The Music's Over

Vinny took the steps to the upper level two at a time. His palms were slick from playing and slipped on the metal railing, threatening to send him tumbling backward to the stage. He hit the mid-way platform, bounding up the last dozen steps to the top.

Ritchie Smith stood atop a tower of speakers, looking out on Maracana Stadium, the audience of eighty-thousand roaring approval.

What happened to the twenty-minute break between acts? Everything was crazy tonight and Vinny wondered how much was due to Howard's absence. With Howard gone, the whole operation fell apart.

Ritchie spun around, surprised to see Vinny.

"What the hell are you doing here?"

"Have you seen my brother?" Vinny asked.

Ritchie nodded and pointed down the catwalk. It ran through the lighting rigs the entire length of the stage, nearly fifty yards.

This is the same catwalk Evita hanged herself from, Vinny thought. Vance stood at the midpoint, struggling with Bobby Marks' wife and daughter. The little girl gripped the railing with both hands and kicked the back of Vance's thigh. Vance tried to bind Bobby's wife to an X-shaped metal cross hanging beside the catwalk, but she drove a knee into his crotch. Vance doubled over and she kneed him in the face. He rocked back against the railing, making the catwalk sway, then he stood, slapped Bobby's wife across the face, and resumed buckling her ankle to the cross. She kicked his head and face with her free foot.

"Shit!" Vinny said.

"Trish and Pepper are a handful." Ritchie was amused. "You should help your brother."

"No," Vinny said. "I'm setting them free, Ritchie. This has to end."

Ritchie rolled his eyes.

"It's a little late to play hero, Vin," Ritchie said. "End this by helping your brother get Trish and Pepper ready for the blood sacrifice. Do your job, man."

"Fuck this job!" Vinny said. "And fuck you, too. I thought you were Bobby's friend. How can you stand here and watch his wife and daughter... Look at her, Ritchie! She's a *little girl*!"

Ritchie looked away, color draining from his face, shame slumping his shoulders.

"Some songs demand sacrifice," he said. He turned his back on Vinny and faced the Maracana crowd. Thirty feet down, Allen Vent struck a low, droning note on his synthesizer, a sub-audible growl shaking the night.

"You're a piece of shit!" Vinny shouted at Ritchie's back.

"So are you, Vin." The guitarist glanced over his shoulder. "Everything's shit."

Ritchie played a haunting opening run, his fingers flying all the way up the neck of his Les Paul to the thin strings and the tight frets, tweedle-tweedle-tweedle-dee. The show had begun.

Vinny ran down the catwalk toward his brother.

"Vance! Stop!" he shouted. "Let them go!"

Vance ignored him. He nearly had Trish's other leg buckled down, even though she punched him repeatedly in the back of the head. Peppermint kicked Vance's ass and tailbone. Vinny reached them and dragged the little girl away from his brother.

"Stop it, Vance!" Vinny shouted. "What the hell are you doing?"

"The crucifixion! Duh!" Vance slapped Trish's bare stomach, leaving a bloody handprint. The names carved into her skin meant nothing to Vinny. *But they should, dumbass.* The voice in his head belonged to Vance. *Names have power. This is who we work for.*

"Vance, let her go," Vinny said. When had he lost the ability to order his brother around? Once Vance lost his mental illness, he supposed. The little girl kicked Vinny's shin and pain shot up his leg. Her tiny feet felt like stone and Vinny took an immediate liking to Peppermint Patty Marks. Everyone should fight for life with such zest. Vinny doubted he would. The girl kicked him again and he howled.

"Come on, Vance! Enough of this bullshit!" Vinny screamed. "Let her go!"

Vance wrapped his hands around Trish's wrist, trying to get her last limb in the buckle. Trish fought hard—a trio of deep scratches oozed blood down Vance's left cheek. She twisted her body and the crucifix swung away from the catwalk. Vance lost his balance and grabbed the railing to keep from falling to the stage below. Trish punched him in the face. Vance's nose sprayed blood, but he grabbed her arm and forced it toward the buckle.

You can't hurt a dead man, honey. Vinny noticed more

X-shaped crosses hanging from the rafters. *Were these here all through the tour?*

Peppermint stomped the middle of Vinny's foot and bones crunched. He screamed and held the little girl further away. She kicked again, aiming for his balls but connecting with his thigh.

"Vinny," Vance croaked. He worked the final buckle on Trish's wrist. "Take care of Bobby."

Vinny spun around. Bobby Marks stood at the end of the catwalk, a gun in his hand.

Thank God! This is finally over!

"Bobby!" Vinny yelled. He released Peppermint's arm and she kicked his knee so hard, he nearly fell over. Vinny hobbled toward Bobby, hands above his head.

"Bobby! Don't shoot! We'll get your family out of here! Just let me talk to my bro…"

Bobby Marks fired two bullets at Vinny. The first sailed wide. The second pierced Vinny's left bicep. He fell to his knee.

"Ah…Bobby, no!" Vinny held out a hand. Bobby stomped toward him, making the catwalk sway like a funhouse ride. "Please…"

Bobby placed his boot in the middle of Vinny's chest and pushed him off the catwalk.

The fall was bewildering and brief. Vinny landed hard and very, very wrong. He faced up, looking at the catwalk, but his hips twisted around. He couldn't feel anything below his waist.

Cool smoke drifted over the dimly lit stage. Vinny shivered. *You're going into shock.* Vance's voice was so clear, Vinny turned to look for his brother.

Across the stage, Ritchie Smith lay crumpled at the base of the speaker tower, his leg bent at an uncomfortable angle. His Les Paul howled an eerie, almost tuneful feedback. Allen Vent's lifeless body slumped over his keyboards, face replaced with a stringy, red meat mask, dead finger pressing a note that droned on and on.

Where's Vance? Vinny couldn't understand why his twin brother wasn't here. They did everything together...

Coming, bro.

Vance fell from the catwalk and landed beside Vinny with a bone-splintering crunch. The last thing Vinny saw before slipping into beautiful, blissful blackness was Vance's brain leaking onto the stage, oozing out a gaping hole in his ruined skull.

CHAPTER TWENTY

Interlude: Billy, Don't Be A Hero

3

Untermyer Park, Yonkers, New York. July 13, 1977.

"Man, it's hot as balls!" Smoke said, rolling down the passenger window. Humid summer night flowed into the car, not cooling a thing.

"Sorry, man," William said. "AC's not working."

"Why the hell are we driving all the way to goddamn Yonkers on a Wednesday night?" Smoke groused. "I sit in at Basil's on Wednesdays. Missin' that shit."

"You know why we're going to Yonkers," William said. "Are you ready?"

"I play the song same as always," Smoke shrugged. "You're the one with the fancy new part. *You* ready?"

William nodded. They drove the rest of the way in silence. William parked the car on Northern Boulevard and gave Smoke a spare key before they got out.

"What for?" Smoke asked.

"In case we get split up," William said, not meeting Smoke's eyes. He looked ready to jump out of his skin.

"You planning on cuttin' out on me tonight, Deke?"

William shook his head. "No. Just in case."

"I ain't drove a car in years," Smoke said, putting the key in his pocket. "Not sure I remember how."

"There's a train station two blocks east if you're more comfortable with mass transit," William said.

"What's this about, Deke?" Smoke gave William a jaundiced gaze. "You got something else in mind 'sides what we got planned?"

"No," William said. "I'm just trying to cover all the bases, okay?"

"You look nervous, man," Smoke said. "Like you're getting ready to bolt."

"I'm not going anywhere," William said. "But I don't know what's going to happen tonight, Smoke. I *think* I know, but it's never been done before, never even been *attempted*, as far as I know. We're breaking new ground, going up against some old, *old* ways."

"That's what artists do, Deke. You plan, create, and improvise when shit goes sideways," Smoke said. "Listen, I'm a roadhouse hack. I got a few chops, but I ain't nothing special. But we got a chance to do something amazing tonight, Deke. Sing the beast to bed and close up that nasty hole in the sky. Finally kill the ghosts been hauntin' us for so long."

William nodded.

"Let's do it," Smoke said. "If we get back by ten, I can catch the last set at Basil's."

The entrance to Untermyer Park was overgrown, but easy to find, situated between two stone pillars. The park was dark until William and Smoke walked in a ways and saw a ring of torches. Two low-top spinet pianos sat side-by-side on a plywood stage, metal folding chairs arranged in front to accommodate a fairly large audience, though

Smoke didn't see any people.

David rushed out of the darkness, his face shiny and eager.

"You're here! Oh, I'm so happy you're here!" David shook Smoke and William's hands, his palms sweaty.

"Where is everyone?" William asked. "We were told this was a party."

"Oh, it is! It is! Come." David led them along a path away from the stage. Smoke's boots crunched over broken beer bottles and discarded needles.

David took them up a rocky path to a domed structure made of ornate stone columns. People gathered in small clusters in the darkness and Smoke sensed more eyes watching from the woods. Every group they passed stared and fell silent, whispering behind their backs. *That's right, assholes, the musicians are here*. Most appeared dressed for a concert, in shorts and T-shirts. A few wore three-piece suits despite the oppressive heat and several dressed in long, heavy ceremonial robes. *It must be* terribly *hot under there.* They passed the body of a slaughtered animal, a goat or a dog, split wide open on the rocks, its insides arranged in strange patterns.

Robert and Mary Ann greeted them beneath the dome. Both looked intimidating in their red velvet robes, yet soggy and wilted from the heat. The dome overlooked the Hudson, moonlight twinkling on the water, but the surrounding gardens were weedy, Greek columns covered with graffiti, floor littered with trash and old blankets. Smoke got the impression they had invaded a homeless person's living space.

"Gentlemen!" Robert spread his hands wide. "Welcome to the Temple of Love! Now that you're here, our evening can begin!"

Robert led them back down the stone path, scowling at

the animal sacrifice as they passed.

"I don't know *why* they insist on doing that!" Robert sighed. "It's disgusting, cruel, and pointless, especially if you don't know how to perform the ritual correctly. These amateur clowns did *not*."

Robert pointed to a pentagram drawn in animal blood and shook his head in dismay. He led them along a path through the woods, and Smoke heard people moving through the trees along with them. It sounded like a lot of people, but the darkness hid their true numbers.

"We have a lot of visitors with us tonight," Robert spoke so only Smoke and William could hear. "Out-of-towners, some important to our mission, others not. Word of your performance spread quickly and everyone wanted to be here. I couldn't say no. That would be rude. So while you're here as guests of The Process, I need you to understand not everything you see and hear tonight necessarily reflects our organization's beliefs."

"Crazies in the house," Smoke said. "I've played those gigs before. Often, actually."

Robert nodded and leaned in close.

"Those Ordo Templi Orientis assholes get out of control every year and clog the Port-a-Johns," he whispered.

They arrived at the stage, Smoke surprised to find an opening act. Three nude men sat cross-legged, playing crude-looking bongo drums. The skin on the drum heads looked supple and human. Mary Ann de Grimston stepped out on stage topless. Smoke enjoyed the heavy sway of Mary Ann's breasts, but didn't much care for how she painted her body with red, squiggly symbols and names…those damned *names*…

"I'm nervous!" Robert said. David stood behind Robert and put a hand on de Grimston's shoulder in a way Smoke found oddly familial.

"Everything will be fine," William said, but Smoke heard tension in the younger man's voice. *He's thinking about his father...his son...* William's nerves were contagious and butterflies took flight inside Smoke's stomach. *It's just another gig, man. Relax.*

They waited until Mary Ann finished singing and chanting with the drummer boys and Robert led them up the stage steps. Ice-water dread filled Smoke's stomach. William looked pale and sweaty. *Will the kid be able to play?* Smoke performed for plenty of rough crowds, but tonight's audience was truly wicked, the bad vibes palpable.

Mary Ann and the drummers left. No one applauded, but Smoke got the impression it would be inappropriate, as if this were more a mass than a concert.

Robert welcomed the crowd, promised to keep his comments brief and spent the next seven minutes thanking a number of groups, organizations, and individuals Smoke never heard of. Smoke and William sat awkwardly at their pianos waiting for Robert to finish. Smoke ran his fingers over the old Baldwin. The keys felt like real ivory.

"We're all here to listen to these two gentlemen perform a very special piano arrangement, so I won't keep you waiting any longer," Robert finally said. "These men probably need no introduction. I had someone say to me this week, 'I didn't think Smoke Johnson was real. I thought he was a myth, a legend.' Well, let me tell you, Smoke Johnson is most definitely real, most definitely a legend, and he is here to play for us tonight, along with the legendary Billy Deacon! Gentlemen, the stage is yours."

Robert stepped away from the microphone, and the crowd applauded despite itself. Someone unleashed a bloodcurdling scream. Smoke played the opening run, getting a feel for the keyboard, letting the notes float gently into the night. The audience fell silent, the only other sound beside Smoke's piano, the low, moaning horn of a tug boat somewhere far north up the river and the call of night creatures along the Palisades.

Smoke let the song unfold slowly, naturally, like a falling leaf, the whisper of panties hitting the floor, the sound of the sun sinking over the horizon. Gravity kept the world spinning and worked in tandem with Smoke's fingers and feet, the ivory keys, felt hammers, taut strings, all falling, falling, falling into place. He gave himself over to the song, poured himself into it, and the song took him willingly in its lover's embrace, eager to bloom beneath Smoke's fingertips.

William joined in, doubling Smoke's part. Smoke glanced over and flashed William a yellow smile, but William focused on his piano, sweating dripping down on the keys. He looked sick and a few notes rang sour. *Kid ain't gonna make it.*

Flashes of heat lightning illuminated the summer night, low, dark clouds coalescing over Untermyer Park. A hot wind bent trees in half and someone (something) howled like an animal. Dark mist rose from the audience and turned into flying nightmares with black mouths and sharp teeth. Screams joined the howls. A creature with a hundred red eyes and a thousand snake-like arms rose from the Hudson and scaled the cliffs of the Palisades with alarming speed, its slimy limbs slithering through the park, lined with hungry mouths. A beast with the head of a jackal and the body of a man danced off to the right of the stage, and several audience members twisted their bodies into pretzel-like poses. William pounded his piano harder and the music sailed on the hot New York night.

The song circled around to its starting point, but William changed his part, meeting every note Smoke played with a counternote that turned the song around, shading light notes dark and turning the dark to light. No matter how subtle Smoke's phrasing, or how swiftly his hands moved over the keyboard, William matched him note-for-counternote, changing the song from a war march to a spiritual anthem, a song of man, not monsters.

The dark shapes in the sky swirled in confusion, absorbing each other, tearing one another to smoky shreds. A bolt of lightning struck an ancient oak near the stage. The massive tree toppled, missing the stage, but crushing several people. It burst into flames, incinerating half the audience in a flash of white-hot fire. Lightning struck again, further south, and Smoke watched half the lights of New York City wink out.

The beast from the Hudson flailed its thousand arms, cutting through the remaining audience members like hungry whips, slicing people in two and slithering back around to feast on the steaming innards. It beat its limbs against the ground and the earth shook so violently, Smoke feared Untermyer Park might tumble off the cliff and into the river.

Smoke and William played on. William tossed his head back, face to the sky, eyes filled with an eerie, unearthly light. He returned Smoke's smile, but William's mouth was so wide and twisted, his eyes so alive and filled with unspeakable knowledge, Smoke pissed himself with terror, a spurt of urine streaming down his leg.

The front of Smoke's piano exploded in a shower of splintered wood. Stunned, Smoke looked down at his fingers and something whizzed overhead, close enough to make his scalp tingle.

David stood in front of the stage, amid a field of blood and wrecked bodies, the smoking barrel of his gun pointed in Smoke's direction. He fired again. Smoke dove beneath his piano, but the shot went wide, the bullet flying into the dark.

"Liars! Betrayers!" David shouted. He fired another round. Splinters of wood burst from William's piano.

"Deke! Get down!" Smoke yelled.

David's next shot hit William in the shoulder, and William's left hand fell dead on the keyboard with a low rattle of notes. But his right hand played on, William's face twisted in pain, fingers wrenching every note he could from the piano.

"Get down, you damn fool!" Smoke crouched into a tight ball behind his piano.

David fired again and the bullet struck William in the chest, toppling him backward off the piano bench. The music stopped and a strange hush settled over Untermyer Park. The shadow people faded and the monster crawled back into the Hudson, its thousand arms undulating like sea grass before sliding beneath the dark waves.

"I thought you were my friends!" David shouted before running off into the night.

Smoke crawled over to William. Blood bubbled from his chest wound, ran down William's sides. Smoke looked around for help—Robert, Mary Ann, anybody. They were all gone, the park suddenly empty except for sliced, half-eaten bodies. The fallen oak burned on, casting everything in a flickering orange glow.

"Hang in there, Deke," Smoke said.

"Fuck, Smoke," Deke said. "It's bad."

"Lotta blood, but we'll get you stitched up, man." Smoke found a cloth cover beneath one of the pianos. He wrapped it into a ball and pressed it against William's chest. The cloth soaked through in seconds. Smoke folded William's good arm across his chest.

"I'm gonna get you out of here, Deke," Smoke said.

"Fuck it, Smoke," William said. "I'm a goner. You go."

"I'm going to pick you up and get you on your feet," Smoke said. "I need you to walk out of here."

"It's too late, Smoke."

"Come on now. Work with me. We can't wait for an ambulance." Smoke pointed to the sky. Another lightning bolt struck near Manhattan. "We gotta get out of here, Deke. I think we pissed something off."

"Tell my wife I love her," Deke said. "My boy...my boy..."

"Screw that. Tell them yourself," Smoke said. He lifted William onto the piano bench, repositioned himself, and helped William stand. William screamed and moaned, but got his feet under him.

"I'm never going to make it, Smoke," he said.

"Hardest part is getting back on your feet," Smoke said. "It's gravy from here. Come on."

Smoke helped William off stage and along the walkway. Darkness raced in once they left the glow of the fire. *Stay on the path, Smoke. It'll take you out of here.* William's blood felt warm and wet on his shoulder.

"Leave me..."

"Shh!"

They shuffled down the wooded path, the only sound their labored breathing and the scrape of William's foot on the concrete. Something rustled in the brush behind them.

"Come on, Deke," Smoke said, quickening his pace. "Let's pick it up a little."

"Can't," William grunted. Every step brought wincing agony, every breath a gasping sob. "Just...leave..."

"Shut up, fool!" Smoke broke into a trot, but William nearly toppled over so they slowed down again. The woods stirred around them. Smoke couldn't turn around, but thought he heard footsteps. Smoke had no way of knowing how far they were from the street until he and William staggered past the stone pillars guarding the park entrance, leading them back to Northern Boulevard. The street was dark, yet alive with activity. Car headlights poked holes in the dark, along with flashlights and fires. So many fires. Breaking glass echoed in the night.

"Shit, William," Smoke said, drag-carrying William along the sidewalk to the rusty Pinto. He leaned William against the side of the car. William slumped over, moaning. Smoke got him upright again and searched his pocket for the key. Blood made his hands sticky, but Smoke found it. His hands shook so badly, it took him several tries to unlock the door.

"It's a blackout, Deke," Smoke said. He swung the passenger door open with a squeak and helped William into the seat. William screamed when he sat down, and blacked out.

"Deke!" Smoke slapped his cheek. William came around, but his gaze remained unfocused.

"I'm gonna get you to a hospital, Deke," Smoke said. He kept talking even after he slammed the passenger door and circled around to the driver's side. "Just be cool, man. Be cool."

A tree limb fell on the roof of the car with a thunk and then rolled over to reveal a line of gnashing, toothy mouths. Smoke jumped in the driver's seat and slammed the door, locking it behind him. He leaned over and locked William's door too, even though he didn't think the creature could work the handle.

The limb slammed down on the Pinto's roof with such force, a zig-zag crack appeared on the windshield. It slithered across the hood, mouths yawning wide as they slid over the cracked glass.

"Fuck!" William yelled and Smoke was glad to hear

from him. Smoke twisted the key in the ignition and the Pinto sputtered to life. The limb reared for another strike. Smoke slammed the car into drive, cut the wheel, and floored it. The limb clipped the back bumper and the Pinto spun, but Smoke cut the wheel and got back on Northern Boulevard. He pulled onto Route 9A, but the roadway hugged the edge of the water, and Smoke kept looking out the passenger window to see if the river monster followed. He cut over to Route 95 at the George Washington Bridge and crossed over to the Harlem River Drive, thinking the East River safer.

"Damn, we should have gone to Jersey!" Smoke said. "Look at this shit!"

Darkness blanketed New York City. The only light came from fires—they burned everywhere...apartments, storefronts, even in the middle of cross streets—emergency vehicles flashing red and blue as they sped through the unlit streets. Inky people moved in the shadows, reminding Smoke of the song's dark, swirling fans.

"Did we do this, Deke?" Smoke asked. "Is this our fault?"

"We did it, Smoke," William mumbled, but it sounded like he was talking about something else, maybe tonight's performance.

"We sure did, Deke. We sure did," Smoke said, but it felt like a lie after the sea monster attack.

William didn't answer. *Was he still breathing?* Smoke slapped his face again.

"Deke! Come on! Snap out of it!"

William's head lolled to one side.

Smoke found Lenox Hill Hospital by following an ambulance, but emergency vehicles clogged 77th Street. As he waited for a break in the traffic, people pelted the

Pinto with bricks and bottles. The rear passenger window shattered and Smoke was forced to back out. He traveled south down Second Avenue, but New York-Presbyterian and Bellevue were also swamped.

"We should get us a room at the nut hut, Deke," Smoke said. "But it looks like they're all booked up tonight."

Smoke circled the Bellevue block twice until a man with a tire iron and a face full of hate chased them away. The deeper they traveled into Manhattan, the more chaotic things became. A gang of people tossed a mailbox through a department store window on First Avenue. The horde rushed in, emerging moments later carrying televisions and stereo equipment. A woman with a baby sat screaming on the sidewalk while people with flashlights strolled by, eyeing her like a curiosity or a freakshow amusement. Every storefront between 23rd street and 14th street appeared burning. Smoke jammed on the brakes to avoid two men fighting in the middle of Third Avenue. Somebody banged on the passenger window and jiggled the door handle, trying to get in. Smoke floored the gas pedal, clipping one of the street fighters with the rear of the Pinto, sending the man sprawling.

"Good Lord, the city's gone mad, Deke," Smoke said. William didn't answer.

Smoke finally got help at Beth Israel Medical Center near Union Square. He pulled the Pinto right into the ambulance bay, jumped out, and screamed until two interns with flashlights came to whisk William away. He hadn't drawn a breath in an hour. A girl with a clipboard told Smoke he needed to talk to the police after he moved his car. Smoke backed the Pinto out of the ambulance bay and drove around the darkened city until dawn, slowing occasionally to watch a fight or a fire. A fleet of stolen

Pontiacs whizzed past him in Brooklyn, MSRP stickers gleaming white, drivers hanging out the windows, howling into the steaming night. *Is this the new world, or the old one showing its true colors?*

Smoke parked in Port Authority after sunrise and waited in the dark terminal for a bus to anywhere.

4. *Bob's Shoe Shine and Moonshine, Gillsburg, Mississippi. October 20, 1977.*

Everything went to shit after July.

Electricity returned to most of New York by July 14, but the city still sweltered under a staggering crime and economic crisis.

Robert and Mary Ann de Grimston eventually reformed The Process Church and several years later it evolved into Best Friends Animal Society. Robert always had a soft spot for animals.

Stricken by Smoke and William's betrayal, David lost his will to live. Even hunting lost its joy. He tried once more, on the last day of July. David opened fire on Stacy Moskowitz and Robert Violante, both twenty years old, while the couple necked in a car in Brooklyn's Bath Beach neighborhood. Moskowitz died. Violante recovered, but was left nearly blind. Dozens of witnesses saw David commit the crime. Sloppy, sloppy, slop-slop. New York City police arrested him ten days later.

Smoke lost the will to play. He headed south, but didn't play another gig until August 15 at Polk's Pit Stop in Nashville and only then because he ran out of cash. He played the song deep into the third set, coming out of a Motown medley, when the bar was nearly empty. He played it slow and sad and tried to stick in as many of William's parts as he could remember. The air shimmered with spirits, but the shadow people were unusually pensive.

Elvis Presley died in one of Graceland's many bathrooms the following day.

Smoke kicked around the South for several months, picking up joyless gigs on the old circuit here and there. He longed to rid himself of the song. Maybe he could give it away—let some other schmuck feed and care for it.

Smoke smoked behind a tiny club called Bob's Shoe Shine and Moonshine in Gillsburg, Mississippi. It was October 20, but the nights were still mild in Mississippi. He stared at the moon and imagined William's mad-smiling face embedded in the stars. *Miss you, Deke!* Smoke tossed his cigarette in a puddle of mud and went inside to play the night's final set.

The song blossomed naturally from a Cole Porter tune and Smoke let it come, welcoming its cold, familiar embrace and the memories of William's crazy face and flying fingers trying, trying, trying to put the world right. Smoke poured himself into the song, let it flow through him, becoming his own song of loss and sorrow. The shadow creatures swirled and feasted with a respectful reverence as Smoke's song drifted into the night air. It's not a bad song, if you know how to use it. A private jet flying high above Bob's Shoe Shine and Moonshine experienced sudden engine failure and crashed in the woods about five miles north, killing four members of Lynyrd Skynyrd's band and crew.

Some songs demand sacrifice.

CHAPTER TWENTY-ONE

The Show Must Go On

Vinny opened his eyes.

Howard Phillips hovered above him, a thin, chipmunk-cheeked angel.

Vinny closed his eyes and wished Howard away. *He'll be gone when I open my eyes again. This is a bad dream— the gunshots, the fall, Vance's leaking brain.*

Instead the faces of William Deacon Jr. and his grandfather appeared alongside Howard's. Vinny didn't recognize the Deacons at first. They'd ditched their expensive suits in favor of crushed velvet robes the color of dried blood. Red stripes decorated their faces, one under each eye, two along each cheek, not paint, but peeled strips of skin. Everybody pitched in for tonight's blood sacrifice.

"What do we do now?" William Jr. sounded nervous.

"You promised the Infinitus would open this evening, Howard," William Sr. growled.

"With all due respect, William, there's no way we could have predicted Bobby's actions tonight," Howard said.

"You assured us Bobby Marks was under control," William Sr. said.

"He *was* under control, until you dragged his wife and daughter into this," Howard said.

"We all agreed it was the best way to complete the Infinitus ritual," William Jr. said.

"I told you Bobby would become unpredictable when you added his family to the equation," Howard said.

"You didn't predict he'd bludgeon his goddamn bandmates to death!" William Sr. said.

"No, I didn't, William. No one could have predicted that. I don't see how arguing about it is going to solve the problems at hand."

The three men stared down at Vinny.

"Will he live?" William Jr. asked.

"Can he play?" William Sr. asked.

"Yes, yes. Corba can fix him," Howard said.

"Are you sure? Once the song begins it must be completed," William Jr. said.

"I know how it works, Billy," Howard said. "Vinny's not the one I'm worried about."

The three faces hovering over Vinny looked off to the left.

"How's he doing?" William Jr. asked.

"There's a lot of tissue loss." Corba's voice came from nearby. "This is…bad. There's not much left to work with."

"He didn't have much to begin with," Howard said. "But we don't need much. Even lower brain functions will suffice."

"I'll do my best," Corba sighed. "No promises. He's…missing a lot."

"Do your best, but do it quickly," Howard said. "What about Ritchie?"

"No," Corba said. "Too much internal hemorrhaging."

"Dammit! You can't keep him going for twenty minutes?"

"No," Corba repeated. "I told Six-Pack and Pike to put him up with the others."

"Shit. I don't know if these two assholes will be enough," Howard muttered, glancing at Vinny. He called to someone off stage. "Bring the crate!"

"You sure?" William Jr. asked. "We didn't factor in…"

"We have to pull out all the stops," Howard said.

"Is Thom ready?" William Sr. asked.

As if on cue, Thom Thomas launched into his unmistakable, lead-footed beat. The stage vibrated beneath Vinny's back. Thom played a hybrid tempo, halfway between Mick The Stick's frantic beat and Thom's original "Summoning Song" groove. Thom's beat made music of the droning keyboard and screaming guitar feedback and the audience cheered. Allen Vent and The Strange Creations didn't have a curtain, but billowing clouds of fog and dry ice blocked the audience's view of the stage.

"Help me get him up," Howard said. With Corba's help, they lifted Vinny to his feet. His arm and hip flared with pain and Vinny blacked out. He came around in Corba's arms, Howard slipping his bass guitar over his head. Vinny tried to take the instrument off, but his arms were too weak.

"Leave it on, Vin," Howard said. "You'll be strong enough to play in a minute."

"I'm…not…" Vinny said, but his mouth filled with blood and he spat out a wad of red phlegm. Something inside felt broken. "I'm not playing shit."

"This isn't the time to take a hero's stand, Vin," Howard said. "Play the song and you'll *be* a hero. Your name will go down in history."

"As the man who killed the world," Vinny said. "No thanks."

"History is written by the winners, Vinny," Howard said.

"Play for the winning team. *Play!*"

"No," Vinny said.

"What about your brother?" Howard said. "He needs you, Vin."

Vance hunched behind Allen's keyboards. The left half of his skull was missing, only one bleary pupil visible beneath a thick layer of bandages.

"Good God," Vinny said. "What have you done to him?"

"This was Bobby's fault," Howard said. "Corba did his best, but your brother...well, frankly, your brother needs to stop getting shot in the head. His ankle is twisted from the fall, but we'll wrap it properly after the show. Same for your hip—Corba thinks you may have a fracture, but we won't know until you get an x-ray. You'll be fine. Corba gave you both something to ease the pain and help with your coordination. It should take effect soon."

Vinny clenched his fingers and the gauze around his upper arm seeped red.

"Don't make a big deal, Vin," Howard said. "The bullet passed right through the meat and out the other side. It's barely going to leave a scar."

He tried taking his bass off, surprised he could lift the instrument as high as his shoulder, but Howard stopped him again.

"Big audience tonight waiting to hear their favorite song, Vin," Howard said. "Go ahead. Play it. Play it and change the world."

"No," Vinny said. "Stick magic beans in The Strange Creations and make them play it."

"I'm afraid it's a little late for that," Howard said. "Bobby Marks has left the building, as they say, taking tonight's blood sacrifice with him. He was kind enough to leave his bandmates behind, however."

Howard pointed up. Allen Vent, Mick the Stick, and

Ritchie Smith hung from metal crosses suspended above the stage. Mick and Allen showed signs of severe head trauma (there was a bloody hole where Allen's face used to be), and one of Ritchie's feet twisted backward. Loops of intestine spilled from their sliced bellies, hanging past their toes. The trio of dead musicians resembled a grotesque Christmas decoration, glittering red and silver above the lighting rig.

"Triple crucifixion instead of a double, *and* the better band gets to play," Howard smiled. "All's well that ends well. Sometimes complex problems have a way of working themselves out."

"That's fucked," Vinny said.

Howard didn't dignify his comment with a response.

Vance played a simple, child-like melody on the keyboard, testing his reanimated hands. The audience cheered.

"Come on, Vin! The band's all here!" Howard stepped aside so Six-Pack and Pike could push a wooden crate onto the middle of the stage. The security guards were splattered with blood, and, it appeared to Vinny, specks of their own vomit

Where the hell were you earlier? You *were supposed to handle Trish and Peppermint, not Vance and I!* Six-Pack stared a thousand yards away, while Pike sobbed loudly, face streaked with tears. They'd had a rough night, too.

They lifted the lid off the crate and the four sides fell. Smoke Johnson stood in all his smoky glory. The first few rows began to chant.

"Smoke, Smoke, Smoke…"

Thick fog blanketed the stage and the lights remained dim. Vinny wasn't sure how the fans even saw Smoke. Perhaps they *sensed* him. Smoke resembled a blackened pretzel as he crossed the stage to a weathered upright piano. The chant traveled the stadium floor and within minutes all of Maracana took it up.

"Smoke, Smoke, Smoke, Smoke…"

Smoke lowered himself onto the bench and played a short, fast run to loosen up his charred fingers. The crowd roared.

"He's got quite a fan club," Vinny said.

"You have no idea," Howard said. "Smoke is beloved in this world and beyond…except by those who hate him. Ready?"

"No," Vinny said. "Get it done as a three-piece. I'm out."

"Can't do it, Vin," Howard said. "The song demands your spirited bass playing…as well as your brotherly love and beating heart. Our research shows at least half of the musicians at an Infinitus opening must be alive and breathing or it won't work. Believe me, we tried your Jimi Hendrix/Keith Moon suggestion long ago and it was a disaster. Summoning the Great Ones with dead meat is a terrible offense, apparently. It's also hard to find live musicians who are comfortable performing with dead ones. There's still a bias, even in this enlightened day and age."

"You're insane," Vinny said.

"I want you to be happy, Vinny. I want you to look forward to the future," Howard said. "The Deacons have agreed to bring Evita back."

Vinny stared at Howard. How could he believe such a seasoned liar?

"See for yourself, Vincent." Howard pointed stage left. The Deacons stood on either side of a hooded figure slouched in a wheelchair. Dr. Corba stepped behind the chair and pulled the hood back. Evita's features were no less lovely in death. Vinny longed to kiss her scorched, blistered cheeks, run his fingers through her brittle hair.

Corba made sure Vinny saw the magic bean between his thumb and forefinger. He tilted Evita's head forward and worked the base of her skull with an enormous knitting needle.

"The reanimation process has begun, Vinny...I call it the Herbert West Express!" Howard slapped Vinny on the shoulder, causing Vinny's gunshot wound to flare with pain.

"Evita can't come back until she hears you play," Howard said, cupping his ear with his palm. "Listen, Vinny. Your band awaits! Join them!"

Vance and Smoke toyed with the melody, tossed it back and forth, coming close enough to make the air shimmer and steam. Thom stuck to tasteful high-hat and cymbal work, with only the occasional crack of the snare or thump of the kick to hint at his underlying power. Vinny never heard Thom play with such restraint or finesse.

Howard tip-toed into the wings, where the Deacons stared at Vinny, faces full of child-like expectation. Corba stepped back, tilting Evita's head upright.

Evita's eyes snapped open, causing a tiny avalanche of black ash to tumble down her cheeks. *Those eyes.* Even filmed-over, fixed and dilated, they offered such promise, such hope. Such love.

Vinny wrapped his fingers around the neck of his bass and stepped centerstage, ready to play his heart out.

CHAPTER TWENTY-TWO
Watkins Glen Jam

Vinny plucked his first note—a fat, round G—and the stage lit up, flash-pots exploding. Maracana Stadium erupted. With Vance and Smoke pinned behind pianos and Thom tucked away behind the drums, Vinny had the stage to himself. He prowled its full length, popping the bass with his thumb, adding some much needed funk and grind. The entire stadium swayed as one to Vinny's groove, except for the fans twisted into strange, Satanic yoga shapes. Vinny felt like a god.

Evita stirred in her wheelchair and Vinny's heart leapt in his chest. Giant video screens behind the drum kit magnified the stage and Vinny saw himself reflected there, smiling like a goon. The Deacons relocated to the drum riser; William Jr. stood to the left of Thom, William Sr. on the right. They played tympani with large wooden mallets, doubling Thom's beat. The video captured a close-up of the Deacons, the resolution high enough to see faded tattoos, patches of hair, and the etched names of the Great Ones (*the names, always the names*) on the drum skins.

Vinny couldn't see much of Thom beyond a quivering mass of flesh behind the kit. Vance's bandaged head tilted to the side, his smile wide, a line of drool connecting his slack jaw to the keyboard. Smoke rocked in time with the music and, despite the volume, Vinny heard the burnt corpse's terrible laugh.

A smattering of crowd surfers sailed over the undulating sea of hands, a group of three bobbing closer and closer to the stage. It was Bobby Marks and his family. They bled from freshly carved cuts (*the names, always the names*). The little girl screamed. Her mother looked dead, passed limply atop the crowd. Bobby fought his way across the sea of waving arms, grabbing his wife's hand and crawling forward to reach his daughter. *Almost there, Bobby. Keep fighting.*

Terrible, flying nightmares, with long, needle-like teeth, flew in erratic, zig-zag patterns around the stadium, pausing here and there for a bite. Snakes and frogs rained from sky and the earth cracked open, emitting sulphuric smoke. The stage heaved beneath Vinny's feet and the lighting rig swayed above him. *It's an earthquake! We're all gonna die!* Vinny burst out laughing, amused by silly thoughts of salvation. The shadow creatures roamed freely through the crowd, dancing wildly and trample-tearing flesh, so red and fresh, an endless source of inspiration. Evita twitched in her chair.

A blur on the video screen made Vinny turn. Howard Phillips stood behind Thom Thomas, holding a sword with a short handle and a long, thick blade. *Where did Howard get a fucking scimitar?* Maybe the Deacons picked one up at the Satanic Warehouse while robe-shopping. Howard Phillips raised the sword above his head.

A blissful smile graced Thom's sweaty face. His arms and legs worked the drum kit like a machine. A dotted line drawn in Magic Marker circled Thom's neck. *Did he draw that himself?* Thom lifted his face toward the rafters, but it was difficult to tell where his thick neck ended and his bloated shoulders began.

Howard Phillips reared back and swung hard, but couldn't sever Thom's head with one blow. The blade stopped three-quarters of the way through Thom's chunky neck and his head flopped backward like a Pez dispenser. Howard needed three more awkward hacks before Thom's head separated from his mountainous body. The cameras didn't pick it up, but Howard appeared to kick Thom's head away in disgust. Howard's crisp suit was streaked with blood, red splatters on his swollen cheek, hair disheveled. Seeing Howard messy unsettled Vinny as much as seeing him run.

Thom kept drumming for a few measures before his arms and legs stopped and his headless torso slumped forward onto the drum kit. The kit toppled off the drum riser with a crash and Thom came tumbling after, spilling to the stage with a massive thump and a splash of blood. The Deacons kept the beat going, mallets pounding stretched human skins.

The moment Thom hit the stage, Evita rose from her wheelchair. She tossed off her robe, gorgeous gown fused to her body like a second skin. She walked to the middle of the stage, charred arms raised to sky.

She's more beautiful than ever!

The sky above Maracana Stadium ripped in half.

It looked fake, the painted backdrop of a middle-school play accidentally torn in half, exposing the darkness backstage. An enormous reptilian arm reached through the hole and groped around blindly, tearing the sky apart further, allowing inky black to flow in and rain down on the Stadium, flooding the field in a pool of nothingness.

A monstrous head made of nightmares, madness, and pure terror burst through the sky. Vinny squeezed his eyes shut to keep them from popping from their sockets. Evita dropped to her knees before the beast.

Vinny scanned the audience for Bobby Marks' family. *Don't look at the sky! Don't look at it!* Trish and Pepper floated atop the crowd a few feet from the stage. Trish appeared unconscious, Pepper wide-eyed with fear, helpless and adrift on a sea of hands. The crowd surged forward and Trish and Pepper tumbled on stage like flotsam. The little girl wouldn't release her father's hand, but the crowd wouldn't let go of Bobby Marks either. Love and fear flashed in Bobby's eyes.

The fans pulled in opposite directions and Bobby Marks tore apart like a piñata, bursting into a red cloud. Pepper fell back to the stage, still clutching his arm, torso, and his left leg to the knee. The crowd fought over the rest, batting Bobby's head around like a beach ball, his face frozen with a look of eternal surprise.

Pepper saw everything. She screamed and huddled against her mother in the middle of the stage.

"It's okay! I'll get you out of here!" Vinny shouted, but the girl flinched away, pulling the ruined torso of her father over her like a security blanket. Vinny was in no position to make promises and Pepper knew it.

"Pepper! Pepper! I can't see!" Trish screamed.

"I'm here, Momma."

"Is your father here?"

"He's…he's with us, Momma."

Vinny lifted his bass over his head and tossed it away, the song finally through with him. Vance and Smoke played on, Vance's smile wide and drooling, Smoke's as bright and yellow as the sun. The Deacons played on too, though William Sr. looked ashen and ready to fall over. The video screens fizzled out and one toppled backward, crushing several crew members. Howard Phillips was nowhere in sight.

"Evita!" Vinny shouted, but she didn't hear him. She knelt at the edge of the stage, watching the world end. Maracana Stadium split down the middle and bodies rained down from the upper deck like autumn leaves. The statue of Christ the Redeemer toppled as the mountain beneath it stood and stamped its tectonic feet like an angry child. The exits clogged with crushed bodies.

"Evita," Vinny screamed again. "We have to get out of here!"

She continued to ignore him. The Great Reptile In The Sky raked its scaly claw over the crosses dangling above the stage, making Allen Vent and the crucified Creations spin and twinkle like wind chimes. Allen Vent lost his guts completely, intestines hanging all the way to the stage, leaving wet, red squiggles on the plywood.

The beast swatted the crosses and the entire lighting rig listed forward with a screech of metal. The cable holding Mick The Stick snapped and his cross flew across the stadium like a Chinese throwing star, lodging deep into a pile of bodies blocking one of the mezzanine exits. The two remaining crosses clattered together, severing somebody's leg—Vinny couldn't tell if it was Allen or Ritchie. The bloody limb pinwheeled into the crowd below.

Vinny ran to Evita, wrapped his arms around her from behind.

"We have to go!" He dragged her across the stage to where Trish and Pepper sat. The little girl stared straight ahead but saw nothing, one arm wrapped around her mother's back, the other clutching her dead father's hand.

"Get beneath the drum riser!" Vinny shouted at Trish and Pepper. A door under the riser led to ground level.

Evita grabbed Peppermint and ran. The girl didn't blink,

dragging the remains of her father behind her. Vinny tried to lift Trish up, but she fought him.

"Don't touch me!" Trish screamed. "Where's my daughter? What have you done with her?"

"Your daughter is this way," Vinny pointed. *She can't see, you fool!* "Take my hand and I'll take you to her."

Trish looked scared, uncertain, near panic.

"I'm not holding your fucking *hand*!" she spat. "Give me your elbow."

Vinny led her to the drum riser, detouring around Thom's immense corpse. Evita waited, Pepper beside her. Pepper ran to her mother when Vinny approached.

"Go! Go!" Evita shooed them beneath the drum riser. Pepper stopped short and Trish ran into her back, making them both stumble. Pepper didn't want to run past the scary, burnt lady into the darkness beneath the drum riser. Vinny ran ahead of them to show it was safe.

"It's okay. It's a way out," Vinny explained. He pulled the door open. Red emergency lights illuminated a metal ladder leading down.

Pepper hesitated, looking ready to cry.

"Please, it's the only way out of here," Vinny said.

Trish gave Pepper a nudge.

"Go ahead, honey," she said. "Listen to him."

Pepper ran beneath the drum riser and climbed down the ladder, turning to help her mother once she was at the bottom. Once Trish and Pepper were off stage, Vinny turned to Evita.

"Let's go, my love," Vinny said.

Evita shook her head.

"Your brother," Evita said, pointing toward the stage. Vance and Smoke played a haunting duet beneath the damaged lighting rig.

Vinny shook his head.

"No," he said. "My brother suffered a…a traumatic head injury…..*another* traumatic head injury…he's not himself anymore."

Evita stomped her feet and pointed again.

"Get your brother!" she said. "He'll be crushed…or worse!"

Vinny slipped his arm around Evita's waist, but she sidestepped him. He grabbed her hand, but she slapped it away.

"Go get your brother!" she repeated.

"Look at him, V!" Vinny cried. "Half his head is gone! He's…he's…"

Evita slapped him in the back of the head with surprising force and shoved him out on stage.

"Go!" she pointed, disappearing beneath the drum riser.

She's resurrected five minutes and already she's bossing you around. The voice in Vinny's head belonged to Vance…the Vance of yesterday, the Vance of long ago. *You are one pussy-whipped cuck.*

The sky monster's claw swept toward the stage, fifty yards wide, and Vinny dove flat. The creature grabbed the Deacons with a quick and surprisingly dextrous motion, toppling their tympani off the drum riser. The monster opened its mouth, blotting out the sky, and tossed the Deacons down its gullet, William Jr. and William Sr. superimposed against the infinite black of its throat, like a bad special effect from a low-budget science fiction movie, twirling and tumbling, robes fluttering, growing smaller and smaller until they disappeared completely.

Vinny looked away as the creature closed its mouth. *Don't look at its face! Don't look!* The pores between the creature's scales were as wide as the Maracana's cargo doors and Vinny saw sirens and minotaurs inside, smiling and waving, fighting and fucking. Some pores appeared empty, others clogged with a stinking tar-like substance. Every inch of the massive beast was a nightmare.

Vinny crawled across the stage until he reached Vance's piano bench. He tugged his brother's leg. Vance smiled down at him, drool spilling off the keyboard and splashing the back of Vinny's head.

"Vinny!" Vance exclaimed, his right eye wide with surprise and dull recognition. Everything above Vance's left cheek was gone, including his eye. Corba had packed and wrapped the wound as best he could, but Vance's head still looked like three-quarters of a cantaloupe.

"Vance, let's go," Vinny said.

Vance shook his head.

"Song," Vance smiled. "Pretty."

"The song's over, Vance," Vinny said. He pulled himself up on the piano bench and lifted his brother's hands away from the keys. "All done, Vance. The song is done."

"Song…Smoke…" Vance freed his hand and pointed across stage, where Smoke played on, like Nero, oblivious to the world ablaze around him.

"Let Smoke play if he wants, Vance," Vinny said. "Smoke's…"

Already dead, died on Vinny's lips. *Aren't we all, bro. Aren't we all.*

"Come on, Vance. We need to go, go, go!" The entire stage dropped several inches. A spotlight fell from above, landing with a shower of sparks. Vinny hoped Evita was safe. Trish and Pepper, too. He pulled Vance to his feet, but his brother resisted.

"Smoke…" Vance pointed, dull eye teary and uncomprehending.

"Okay. Smoke too. Damnit," Vinny sighed. "I'll grab his armpits. You take his feet. Carry him under the drum riser and down the ladder. Got it?"

Vance nodded slowly. Too slowly. Vinny repeated the instructions and Vance nodded with more confidence.

"Let's go!"

They whisked Smoke off the piano bench easily, his blackened fingers still twitching in mid-air. Smoke was light as a feather, but his armpits smoldered, blistering Vinny's fingers.

"Put him down! Let him go!" Vinny shouted, prying his brother's fingers away from Smoke's ankles once they were under the drum riser. Blisters covered Vance's palms too, but he seemed oblivious to the pain, staring at Vinny with a cyclopean eye. Vinny spit on his palms and flapped his hands.

"Okay! Down the stairs! Hurry!" A huge crash came from the stage. *There goes the lighting rig.* The right side of the drum riser collapsed, driving Vinny to his knees. *We're not going to make it. It ends here.*

Vance climbed down the ladder. Vinny tried pushing Smoke through the door, but the blackened corpse slapped his hands away. Smoke could climb down himself, thank you. Vinny crawled face-first down the ladder after him…and into Evita's arms.

Even with his feet back on the ground, Vinny didn't want to let her go. He loved the feel of her body in his arms. But Evita pulled away, *ran* away, following Smoke and Vance out from beneath the stage.

The backstage area was empty except for Howard Phillips, hanging out of the door of their tour bus, arms waving. Trish and Pepper (the remains of Daddy at her feet) stood beside the bus, Pepper waving even more emphatically than Howard. *Who's driving the bus? Corba? Pauleo? Donald?* It didn't matter. Howard Phillips was here. Howard had a plan.

Vance reached the bus, but Howard stopped him, letting Smoke board first. Howard shoved Vance hard in the chest, knocking him to the ground. Pepper jumped back in terror, Trish behind her screaming, "What happened? What's going on?"

Howard stepped back onto the bus, the doors slid closed, and the vehicle pulled away. It rolled over Bobby Marks' femur with a violent snap, rattling Pepper's arm in her socket, nearly pulling her off her feet.

"Wait!" Vinny shouted. "What the fuck?"

The bus pulled through the exit doors, turned left, and disappeared, leaving Vinny to pick his half-headed brother out of the dirt, while the stadium—and world—crumbled around them.

CHAPTER TWENTY-THREE
Call Of Cthulu

The fabric of humanity came apart like a stack of newspapers left in the rain, disintegrating into soggy, pulped fiber in minutes.

The moon wobbled in the sky, knocked into an unnatural orbit by a great reptilian beast, an enormous salamander, kicking off its surface. The creature landed in the Pacific Ocean, near the Mariana Trench, causing a string of violent volcanic eruptions, covering much of Asia, India, and parts of Russia with molten rivers of lava and fiery ash. A beast the size of Texas crawled from the Atlantic and swallowed Florida. It ate its way up the coast, nibbling the edges of the continent the way a child nibbles the crust off toast. It devoured Greenland and turned south, taking bigger bites on its return trip.

The Great Ones trampled the earth with feet the size of cities. A snake, as long as the Nile and as wide as Egypt, slithered across the surface of the planet, eating nations, leaving steaming piles of undigested cities in its wake. The Rocky Mountains stood, shrugged off the cities built along its back and stalked toward South America. The Andes rose to meet it and the two ancient ranges fought a great battle. A third mountain range emerged from the Pacific, bigger than the Rockies and Andes combined, and beat them both to dust.

Oceans sloshed over the earth's surface like wine in a drunkard's glass, massive tidal waves washing out the coasts, turning deserts to swamps, burying cities under miles of water. The planet twisted inside as beings long buried fought their way to the surface.

Deep fissures appeared in Northern Russia, near the Arctic Circle, and the steam emerging from the cracks crystalized into an ice beast ten miles tall. It stomped all the way to Moscow and suddenly melted, washing the city away, millions of tiny, pink, wriggling bodies buried in mud and debris.

England and Ireland sunk beneath the waves, undersea kingdoms of drowning sea monkeys. The ocean formed a film of dead meat, a feast for scavengers.

Ticks and jiggers the size of apes and elephants fell from The Great Ones. They had no taste for human flesh, but enjoyed the way it shredded and the endless screams of the tiny people. The military was overmatched by a power beyond comprehension, creatures waiting since the beginning of time for the chance to rise and rule. Nuclear warheads were launched, but swallowed by an enormous turtle that vomited radioactive mucus on its attackers.

Something from the nothing between stars swallowed earth whole, was sickened by its mealy texture and tangy rot, and spat it out again.

The end came to Rio de Janeiro through the hole The Dunwich Horrors (featuring Smoke Johnson) punched in the sky. (In his darkest hours, a darkness borne of his own willful undoing, Vinny considers what he and his brother accomplished with no small amount of pride. *We ripped a fucking hole in the sky.* We *did that!*) The Sky Monster stepped into Maracana, kicking out the stadium's western wall in a cloud of dust and blood. It stomped all over Rio, practically danced on the flattened city, before the Corrado Mountains slapped the creature's nightmarish head off, covering western Brazil in toxic pink paste that ate through metal, stone, and, of course, flesh. Flesh was so very weak.

Six fire-breathing dragons twice the size of commercial aircraft soared through the hole in the sky, flash-roasting whomever remained inside Maracana Stadium. The drum kit burst into flames. The piano strings superheated, screaming as they popped and snapped. A dragon grabbed Thom's headless corpse in its talons, but it was too heavy, and Thom's skin stretched obscenely before breaking with a loud snap, his massive carcass landing on Horrors' fans with a splat. The dragons circled in a widening gyre, breath so hot, it melted glass and steel, liquified blood and bone.

Space spiders followed, ten-legged creatures three times taller than the Rio Sul Center. Sofa-sized lice tumbled free and slid along on trails of slime, seeking new hosts. Anything with warm, wet insides would do.

The Great Ones feasted, frolicked, and fought. Some kicked holes in the world for fun, enraged at being forgotten. Others defended the planet against attackers; they'd waited too long to see their new home ruined by vandals and malcontents.

A living mist made of liquified organic remains and noxious gases settled on the world. A toxic wind circled the planet, seeped into every nook and cranny, bringing gasping, lung-busting death.

There's always a fight, big or small, earthly or unearthly. Swallowed whole or slowly chewed. Digested and absorbed, or spit out and left for scavengers to pick over. Food for something bigger, or something too small, plentiful, and hungry to defend against. Fight and eat, eat and fight, until fighting and hunger are everything, forever.

CHAPTER TWENTY-FOUR
After The Love Has Gone

"Now what?" Evita asked, watching Howard pull away with their bus. The stadium trembled around them with a sound like thunder.

"Come on! The basement is this way," Vinny said. He and Vance smoked a joint there this afternoon, though it seemed a million years ago.

Vinny led Evita, Vance, Trish, and Pepper through a doorway and down a flight of stairs into the sprawl of hallways and rooms below Maracana Stadium. The rumbling overhead sounded like a bowling alley, so they retreated to the quietest corner of the basement. Trish and Pepper set up camp in one of the basement pantries their first night, while Vinny, Evita, and Vance bunked in an empty conference room. Vinny wanted to lay beside Evita, but she moved away every time he did.

"I don't understand...The Great Ones weren't supposed to fight with each other," Evita said, pacing the room.

"Maybe their political system is as fucked as ours," Vinny said.

"No! This...this wasn't supposed to *happen*!" Evita said. "And Howard wasn't supposed to *leave!* Do you think he made it to the rendezvous point?"

"What rendezvous point?" Vinny sighed. "The rocketship to Uranus?"

"Funny, Vin," Evita scowled. "What the hell is that supposed to mean? You want to butt-fuck me?"

"No," Vinny looked into Evita's eyes, so blue and beautiful, yet different... "Didn't we discuss this already?"

"What are you talking about?" Evita asked.

"Thom." Vance pointed to Evita.

Vance's latest head injury limited his ability to speak (and control his saliva). Vinny wondered if Vance also lost his ability to recognize faces...and genders.

"This is Evita, Vance," Vinny said. "Not Thom."

"Thom," Vance said again.

"No. Evita."

"No," Evita said. "Thom."

"What?" Vinny asked.

"I'm Thom," Evita repeated.

"Thom!" Vance shouted triumphantly, drool spilling over his chin.

Vinny grabbed Evita by the shoulders and pulled her close, pressed his lips to hers. Evita pushed him away.

"*Yuck*! Knock it off, Vin!" Evita said. "I told you. I'm Thom. And I don't appreciate your tongue in my mouth...or anywhere else."

"No...it's not possible," Vinny said. "Thom got his *head* chopped off. Howard did it...in the middle of the song!"

"I *told* you the Deacons promised me a new vessel," Evita said. "But I didn't expect them to stick me in this burned-up whore's corpse. This is bullshit! Look! My chest is held together with an old shoelace! I should've stayed fat."

"No..." Vinny said.

"Thom!" Vance repeated.

"Honestly, Vin, the Deacons promised me Vance's

body," Evita said. "But looking at him now, maybe I'm better off. Fuck the Deacons!"

"No. Fuck...*you*!" Vinny jumped on Evita, wrapped his hands around her throat, driving her to the floor. She twisted beneath him, but made no real effort to fight or get away. Vinny throttled her for a full minute, until his hands cramped. Evita wasn't breathing anyway, so he beat the back of her head against the floor tiles.

"Vinny! Stop!" Vance lacked the coordination to pull his brother off Evita, so he threw his body over hers and Vinny finally let go. "Thom! Don't hurt!"

Vinny crawled into a corner, curled into a ball.

"Damn you, Evita...damn you, Howard..." he sobbed. "Damn you all..."

"You're a fucking maniac, Vinny!" Evita said, getting to her feet. "Look at this shit! You cracked my skull!"

Evita wiped the back of her head, showing Vinny and Vance the reddish-black liquid on her fingertips.

"Ouch," Vance said. "Blood."

"Like I don't have enough problems!" Evita shouted, holding the back of her head. "First the Deacons betray me and stick me inside this crispy whore. Then my bandmate goes on a gay rampage and tries making out with me. When I rebuke him, he bashes my fucking head open! Oh, and the world just ended, and we have *no plan*. Zero. *Nada. Nunca.* We are fucking *fucked*!"

Vinny couldn't get off the floor, couldn't stop sobbing. Vance stared at Evita and smiled.

"Thom!" he exclaimed.

"Yeah, Vance...I'm Thom," Evita sighed. "I have to bandage my head. Maybe the girl or her mother can stitch me up..."

Evita left Vinny and Vance alone in the conference room. Vance stood for a long while, watching his brother cry. He sat next to Vinny and rubbed his brother's back. Vance sang "Yesterday," Vinny glad his brother's voice still sounded strong. He joined Vance on the third verse and felt better by the song's end.

"I don't know what we'll face when we get out of here," Vinny said, looking at the ceiling. "But we'll face it together, okay, Vance?"

"Okay, Vinny!" Vance smiled and drooled. Vinny handed him a paper towel.

They found Evita with Trish and Pepper in the kitchen. Vinny explored the adjoining rooms and found cases of bottled water and candy. A deep freezer held boxes of stadium hot dogs and pretzels. *Where's all the beer?*

"At least we're pretty well stocked for a while," Evita said. Vinny nodded but wouldn't meet her eye.

Pepper remained shy and cautious, but was no longer catatonic. Her mother had a harder time. In addition to going blind, Trish's post-traumatic stress left her anxious, fidgety, and barely coherent.

"It swallowed us whole! The monster!" Trish said. "I saw it! I saw its face! Its mouth was bigger than the sky! It ate us up! We're in its belly right now!"

"Monster!" Vance drooled. "Kaiju!"

"Yes...yes! The monster! It tore apart the sky and swallowed us all! The entire planet. We. Are. Eaten!"

"Mom, relax," Pepper said. She touched her mother's forearm and Trish grabbed her daughter's hand.

Evita rolled her eyes, but Vinny couldn't look at her without wanting to kill her...or make love to her.

"Howard Phillips is a double-crossing bastard!" Vinny blurted out.

"Bastard!" Vance echoed.

"He stole Bobby away from me and my daughter!" Trish agreed. "Howard made Bobby play that damned song and it ruined him. It turned him into somebody else. Bobby tried to stop, but he couldn't. He was a good man...the best man...he tried to keep us safe, keep us away. I see that now. Well, actually I don't see anything anymore. Isn't that funny? If your Daddy were here, Pepper, he would have cracked up at that joke. He had a dark sense of humor, but it was wonderful, too. Bobby...oh, Bobby..."

Bobby Marks was an asshole, as far as Vinny was concerned. *Look what he did to Vance's head! I was trying to help him! What a dick!* But now wasn't the time to say anything.

"Howard Phillips betrayed us all," Evita said. "I'm not sure how much he planned and how much got out of hand. I don't think the Deacons or Howard expected the Great Ones to react the way they did. It was our understanding the takeover would be an *ordered* process."

"Deacons!" Vance shouted. "Monsters!"

"What's Howard's plan?" Vinny asked.

"Once the Infinitus opened, Howard, the Deacons, me, and a few others were supposed to board buses and rendezvous in Cascavelo, about three hundred miles southwest of here, on the border of Paraguay." Evita opened her arms wide. *Damn, she's still breathtaking!* "We'd wait in the old mine shafts until the first phase of The Reclamation was complete."

"How long was that supposed to take?" Vinny asked.

"The Deacons weren't sure...six months at least," Evita said. "No matter what method the Great Ones used, there was bound to be decay and general unsanitary messiness for a while."

"Deacons!" Vance said. "Food!"

"There's no air!" Trish screamed so loud, they all jumped...except for Vance, who smiled at nothing in particular. "We won't be able to breathe! We're in the belly of the beast!"

"*Shhh*, Momma!" Pepper said.

"Then what happens?" Vinny asked Evita. "You crawl out of holes in the ground like the Manson Clan and repopulate the earth? You, Howard, and Allen Vent?"

"Not quite," Evita smiled. "We were promised mastery over the remains of humanity. Anyone who survived phase one would be our slaves."

Now that her features matched her psychotic sentiment, Vinny's heart ached for Evita even more. He smiled bitterly.

"But no rocketship to Uranus, huh?"

Evita frowned.

"What the hell does that even *mean*?" she asked. She glanced at Trish and Pepper. "Maybe you shouldn't say."

Vinny shook his head.

"Sorry I attacked you…and bashed your head open," he said. "I wasn't myself."

"Well, I'm not either," Evita said. "I don't know who I am anymore."

"Self!" Vance shouted, pointing to a kitchen shelf.

"We've all…changed," Vinny said, looking from his drooling brother, to mad-blind Trish, to Peppermint, who sat quietly beside her mother, staring at a leaking cloth laundry bag at her feet. A plastic bag would have been a better choice for Bobby's remains…or a garbage can. "None of us are who we once were."

"Thom!" Vance pointed to Evita.

"You ladies are hurt," Evita said to Trish and Pepper. Evita patted the fluorescent orange twine holding the back of her skull together. Vinny couldn't tell if the wide, uneven stitches were made by the child or the blind woman. "You were nice enough to stitch me up. Can I return the favor?"

Trish ran her fingers over the wounds on her abdomen and did the same to Pepper. The oozing cuts formed letters, the letters, names. *Those damned names. Meet the new boss, same as the old boss.*

"No, thank you. They're not deep," she said. "We'll heal."

"At least let me help you clean up?"

"No. My daughter and I can take care of ourselves."

"Listen, the world just got a whole lot smaller," Evita said. "We're going to have to help each other."

Trish hesitated, pulling Pepper closer.

"The Boyle brothers tried to kill us tonight," she said. "How can I trust you?"

"Howard made Vance do that! And I tried to free you!" Vinny said. "Plus, your husband shot us both, so, touché."

Trish smiled without humor.

"How long did you know Bobby?"

"We toured with The Strange Creations for almost two years," Vinny said.

"Did you know Bobby's whore girlfriend?"

Vinny looked at Evita, eyebrows raised.

"We...we knew her," Vinny said. "Bobby...wasn't with her long."

"You must have known what the band was doing." Trish didn't hide the accusation in her voice.

"Monsters!" Vance said, adding with an eerily accurate Japanese accent, "Godzilla!"

"No, not monsters!" Vinny said. "We didn't know there'd be monsters."

"Don't believe them, Mom," Pepper piped in. "They're monsters too. The scary burnt lady and the half-headed man are zombies."

"Is this true?" Trish asked.

"Howard   Phillips   brought   Vance   and   I   back using...supernatural methods," Evita explained.

"You're zombies?" Trish asked.

"Are you going to eat us?" Pepper huddled closer to her mother.

"No. They don't eat people," Vinny clarified.

"Pegdick!" Vance shouted.

"What?" Trish asked.

"Ignore him," Vinny said. "They're zombies, but not the kind that eat people. And Evita...the...the burnt, scary lady...she's got Thom, our drummer, living inside of her."

"The big fat man?" Pepper asked.

"Pepper, that's not nice," Trish said.

"It's okay. It's true," Evita said. "I didn't want to be big and fat, but now I'm burnt and scary. Be careful what you wish for, Pepper."

"Please don't speak to my daughter," Trish said. "You're *all* monsters! You saw what was happening. 'Hangman Jam'...the holes in the sky...what part did *you* play?"

"We were the opening act," Vinny said.

"Yeah. The opening act. Why should I trust you?" Trish repeated. "Why should I believe you?"

Vinny had no good answer. Why does anyone put faith in another in a world full of heartbreak and betrayal? *Because you want to believe. Because you die without hope.*

"You don't have to," Evita said. "But I think we might be the only people left."

"Left," Vance said, holding up his right hand.

CHAPTER TWENTY-FIVE
Incense and Peppermint

The electricity quit after a month, but a back-up generator kicked in, keeping the fridge going and the lights dim. They had enough food and water—a steady diet of ramen noodles and hot dogs—and the air, while increasingly funky, remained breathable.

After a week of confinement, Evita, Vance, and Vinny went on an exploratory mission to the surface. The basement door was blocked from the other side, but a narrow metal utility ladder led through an access panel in the kitchen ceiling to a machine room above. They climbed through the ceiling into a terrible, throat-closing stench, a cloud of sweet decay and rot. Vinny covered his nose and mouth with his shirt, but it didn't help.

Evita eased open the door of the machine room and Vinny peered over her shoulder. The room opened to a large hallway. Flood damage left a line of debris nearly ten feet up the tiled sides of the walls. An apparent cave-in clogged one end of the hallway with rubble. The other end looked clear…except for the giant slugs.

Vinny saw three, each more revolting than the next, pale

white bodies like water balloons the size of taxis. One slug traveled down the middle of the hall, squished flat and round, a humped pancake. Another clung to the wall, while a third crawled upside-down on the ceiling, its shapeless body swaying like a cow's udder. Vinny wanted to puncture it to see what drained out. The slugs slid along on trails of ooze, frequently changing direction. Vinny saw no nose or mouth, couldn't tell which end was which and wasn't sure it mattered. The stench forced Vinny to return to the basement. He immediately puked after climbing down the ladder.

"Sick," Vance said, following his brother down.

"Fuck! That *smell*!" Vinny said, collapsing on a kitchen chair. His stomach lurched again, but he swallowed it down and breathed through his nose. Evita came down the ladder, sliding the access panel closed behind her. The stench clung to her and Vinny moved to a seat across the room.

"I told you it would be bad," Evita said.

"Smell," Vance said, echoing his brother. Vance and Evita lost their ability to detect odors once they stopped breathing.

"What's up with the jumbo slugs?" Vinny said.

"Beats me. Clean-up scavengers maybe. Parasites. Digestive enzymes." Evita looked at Vinny. "Do you think Crazy Trish is right? Are we trapped inside the stomach of something else?"

"How the hell should I know?" Vinny said.

"Monster," Vance said. "Food."

"We're lucky," Evita explained. "We're safe underground and well-stocked, which is better than most. We can ride this out, find Howard, and get my old body back."

"Your old body's got no head...plus, it sucked," Vinny

said. "You were a fat bag of crap. You couldn't even walk."

Nicotine withdrawal made Vinny irritable and a lack of alcohol exacerbated matters. He and Vance found a dusty crate of wine in the back of the pantry, but they'd polished off the last bottle a few days ago and the dryout hit Vinny hard. The pain in his arm and hip subsided, but now it felt like ants crawled beneath his skin. Vance was surprisingly unaffected by nicotine and alcohol withdrawal. Bobby's bullet must have finally managed to remove the addictive part of his brain.

Peppermint spent time with her mother…and father. She boiled and bleached Bobby Marks' skeleton. Only stark white bone and leathery scraps of skin remained. Pepper found a tool box under the kitchen sink and—using glue, screws, and wire—re-assembled her father's bones in unique, non-human ways.

As their third month in the basement began, Vinny tapped Trish on the shoulder. She sat at the kitchen table, face turned toward her daughter. Pepper worked on the countertop, taking her father's bones apart and putting them back together like a macabre erector set.

"Patricia. It's Vinny," he whispered in her ear. "Your daughter is spending an inordinate amount of time with your husband's remains. I'm thinking…maybe we could have a funeral to bring your daughter closure…and we could get rid of Bobby's bones."

"Let my daughter be. She knows what she's doing," Trish said. "Go away."

Everyone grieved differently, Vinny supposed. He tried a direct approach with Pepper a few days later.

"I'm sure you miss your dad," Vinny said. Pepper had Bobby spread over the kitchen table. She'd sewn his scraps of skin together and was reattaching it to his ribs with glue.

She worked with great care and precision, reinforcing Bobby's spine with wire, lengths of broken femur cross-bracing his ribcage. Pepper's grotesque feat of engineering was both impressive and disgusting.

"I know your dad loved you a lot," Vinny said. "He used to talk about you and your mom all the time."

Pepper sensed Vinny's lie and let him know with a quick, hooded stare.

"I...that's an amazing...thing...you're building, Pepper," Vinny said. "But there are other ways to pay tribute to your dad. Like a funeral."

"What instrument do you play?" Pepper asked.

"Uh...I played bass," Vinny said. "Keyboards, too. And viola, and..."

"My father played bass," Pepper said, running her hands over the thing on the table. "Do you have any strings?"

"What? Bass strings? No," Vinny stammered. "Everything...our equipment was destroyed."

Pepper frowned and returned to her work.

"When we get out of here, we'll find you a guitar and I'll teach you to play some of your dad's songs. That would be a better way to remember him," Vinny said. "Listen, Pepper, I know you're hurting and your mom's not in the right frame of mind to tell you otherwise, but you have to get rid of your father's remains. What you're doing is wrong...and gross. A funeral is the way people say goodbye."

"Fuck off," Peppermint said. "Go away."

Vinny pulled back as if struck.

"How old are you?" he asked. Pepper stared at him, eyes wise and weary, practically ancient. Vinny backed away.

Vinny found himself questioning Pepper's age again when a growth spurt left her pant legs six inches shy of her ankles and suddenly she stood as high as her mother's shoulder.

"How old was Peppermint the night of the last show?" Vinny asked Trish. She hesitated. *Does she not remember, or does she not want me to know?*

"Five," she said.

"Looks like she had a growth spurt, Trish," Vinny said. *Keep it gentle...* "She's almost as tall as you now."

Trish cocked her head.

"Pepper. Come here."

Pepper put her instrument aside. *Night and day with that thing!* Trish stood beside her daughter, running her hands over Pepper's body.

"These clothes are tight on you," Trish said.

"I know," Pepper answered. "Maybe I'm eating too many dogs and noodles."

"No...the length...you've outgrown your clothes."

"I'm sorry." Pepper sounded ready to cry.

"It's no big deal," Evita said. "There are sweats and T-shirts in the storage closet. We'll find you something to wear."

"How...how did you get so big, Peps?"

"I don't know, Mom," Pepper said. "I'm sorry."

"I think...time's moving differently," Evita said. "Look at your beard, Vinny! Have you ever grown facial hair like that before in your life?"

Vinny ran his hand over the lush growth on cheeks and neck. No, he and Vance had baby faces, rarely needing to shave more than once a week. But thick whiskers had sprouted from Vinny's face during the last month. Vinny liked his ZZ Top beard, except for the thick streaks of gray.

Trish ran her hands through Pepper's hair and then her own.

"Our hair is definitely longer," she said.

"Everything's sped up," Evita said. "The three of you are aging faster. We notice it more on Pepper because she's a child."

"I'm not a child," Pepper said. "You and the half-headed man don't age because you're zombies?

"Pepper, that's not very nice," Trish said, not sounding like she meant it.

"It's okay," Evita said. "I think she's right. Whatever's happening isn't affecting Vance and me in the same way."

"Is time speeding up, or are we aging faster?" Vinny asked. "Is something in the air? A foreign bacteria or virus?"

"The earth got swallowed," Trish answered. "The planet's out of orbit. Maybe we're moving away from the sun, aging more quickly."

"Well...yeah. Maybe," Vinny said. "But it's more likely Pepper had a normal growth spurt and Trish and I look older because we've been trapped in a basement for four months. It might not be anything at all."

"How will we know for sure?"

They knew for sure a month later when Peppermint got her period.

CHAPTER TWENTY-SIX
We Belong

Peppermint found a stash of old paper maps and a dead flashlight in a kitchen drawer. Vinny sucked at reading maps (and Vance sucked at reading), but Evita figured out the machine room above them wasn't far from the cargo bay where the vehicles were parked. Evita went on a scouting mission and reported the transit van intact but the exit blocked. Evita studied the maps for alternate exits and, after a week of daily exploring, found a drivable route to the stadium parking lot.

"I've been outside," Evita reported. "The sun is gone. The sky is gray."

Vinny collaborated her story the following week. The sun was gone, not covered by clouds, but missing entirely. So were the moon and stars. Day and night were indistinguishable, the landscape cast in permanent twilight. The horizon showed patches of green, pink, purple, and black. Winged reptiles flew in circular patterns at an indiscernible distance (*Christ, are those dragons?*), but Vinny saw no other signs of life. The ground shook (*aftershocks from an earthquake, or the footfalls of a giant?*), but the vibrations faded away.

The compass on the end of the dead flashlight didn't work. The needle never stopped drifting, sometimes changing direction entirely, like the giant slugs in the hallway. Evita tried a trick with a wine cork, a needle, and a glass of water, but it didn't work either—the cork sunk to the bottom of the glass while the steel needle floated on the surface.

"How is that even possible? Where are we?" Evita asked, sounding frightened. The ruined parking lot of Maracana Stadium felt like another planet.

They returned to the basement and Evita hashed out a plan.

"If the roads are intact, we should try to reach the rendezvous point in Cascavelo," she said once they were seated at the kitchen table. "There's still a chance we can catch up with Howard."

"Why should we chase after Howard?" Vinny asked "The guy is a liar."

"He needs to switch me out of this body, for starters!" Evita said. "The Deacons promised…"

"The Deacons got eaten, Evita!" Vinny said. "Their promises aren't worth shit anymore…if they ever were."

"But Howard might have a plan, you know? He always had a plan," Evita said. "And please, call me Thom."

"I want no part of Howard's plans," Vinny said. "Look where they've gotten us."

"You have any better suggestions?" Evita asked. "Where do you want to go?"

"I want to go home," Vinny said, regretting how small and childish it sounded.

"Pegdick," Vance said, surprising his brother.

"Home's gone," Evita said. "All our homes. We need to find a new one."

"We?" Vinny said. "I don't know about that."

"Come on, man! We need to work together!" Evita said. "We can't leave the girls."

"I'm not talking about them," Vinny said.

"Great, Vin. Will you kick me out of the van once it's rolling, or will you abandon me here?" Evita asked. "You're a real prick, Vinny. I helped pull your ass—and your brother's ass—off that stage. You wanted to *leave* him there! You've treated me like shit since I joined the band. What's your problem?"

"I don't have a problem with…you," Vinny said. He rubbed his face with his hands, but it didn't clear the confusion in his mind. "I-I just…I can't take looking at you. I…I loved Evita."

"You dumb ass," Evita sighed. "When will you realize the way people look on the outside isn't who they are inside? I hated being a morbidly obese monster! It was a curse! I was fat at age five and kept getting bigger and bigger, to a point where I was *hiding* inside all that fat. I hated it, but it was better than this!" Evita thumped her stitched-up chest. "At least I had a *heart*! Corba carved Evita's out and gave it to Allen fucking Vent to burn up and chant over!

"But I'm still me, Vin. I'm still Thom," Evita said. "I'm sorry if the way I look upsets you. I'm not fond of it either. But it's not my fault. If we find Howard Phillips, maybe we can fix it."

"You can't go back again," Vinny said, sounding unsure. Evita shrugged.

"So we go forward," she said. "And going forward, can you try not being such a prick? Can we have a new start, Vin? 'Cause, frankly, there's nothing stopping me from taking Trish and Pepper out of here and leaving you and Half-A-Head Vance to fend for yourselves. Girl power!"

Evita smiled and raised a charred fist.

"Half-head!" Vance replied.

"Try it and me and my half-headed brother will kick your fat ass!" Vinny replied. Evita flinched and wrapped her arms around her thin, blackened frame.

"Look, Vin, we have to live together," Evita said. "Can't we get along?"

"Do we have to live together?" Vinny asked. "You don't have to wait. You're free to leave at any time. Go. Catch up with Howard. Crawl in a cozy hole with him. Maybe the rest of us are better off staying here."

Evita nodded and stood.

"Maybe that's for the best," she said, leaving the Boyle brothers alone in the kitchen. Vinny's heart broke all over again watching her walk out the door.

"Thom," Vance said after she'd left. Vinny burst into tears.

"Vinny. Sad," Vance said. He watched his brother cry for a full minute. Vinny stood, walked to the sink, and splashed his face with water. He couldn't stop crying.

"You make me sad, Vance," Vinny said. "Look what's happened to you, bro. Look what you've become."

"Half-head!" Vance smiled. A line of saliva spilled from his lips and ran down his chin.

"Yeah. Half-head," Vinny said. Something big broke inside his chest and Vinny wailed.

"I'm sorry, Vance. I'm sorry I didn't let you go in Panama City. I should have stopped Howard. But I wanted you back, Vance. I couldn't face life without you," Vinny said. "But your head...your whole head...it had a storm raging inside of it that kept getting worse and worse. The medications never really helped...not enough. You were so unhappy for so long...I should have listened to you. I'm sorry I didn't listen closer. I'm sorry I didn't listen *sooner*...I'm *so* sorry..."

"Sorry!" Vance pointed at his brother. "Half-head!"

Vinny searched the kitchens cabinets until he found what he needed—a heavy, black, cast-iron skillet.

"Come here, Vance." Vinny sniffed, skillet dangling from his right hand. "Lean over the sink, bro."

"Sink!" Vance said. He crossed the kitchen and did as his brother asked, bending so far over the sink, his bandaged half-head nearly touched the stainless steel basin.

"I'm sorry, Vance." Vinny took a deep breath and raised the skillet over his head. "I love you, bro."

Vinny swung with all his might. The skillet cracked against Vance's skull and reverberated like a gong. Vance laughed.

This is going to be harder than I thought. Vinny considered cutting the magic bean from Vance's skull, but didn't want to touch it. He needed to smash the skull flat. He raised the skillet over his head again.

"Stop! What are you doing?"

Pepper stood in the kitchen doorway, eyes wide, holding her stained laundry bag in front of her like a shield. Trish stepped behind her, using a yardstick as a cane.

"Don't," Pepper said, assessing the situation with an understanding beyond her years. "Don't kill your brother."

"Please, Pepper," Vinny said. "Go away. This is…this is family business."

"Don't do it, Vinny," Trish said. She pushed Pepper into the kitchen ahead of her. "Your brother is with us."

"My brother is *my* responsibility!" Vinny shouted. "He's *always* been my responsibility. This is what he wants!"

"Are you sure?" Pepper asked.

"Of course!" Vinny said, not sure of anything.

"Vinny!" Vance shouted, still face-down in the kitchen sink. "Mad!"

Evita stepped into the kitchen and crossed the room in a

flash. She yanked Vance out of the sink, away from Vinny.

"What the hell, Vin?" Evita looked like she'd been crying. Dark streaks ran down her sooty face like lava flows. "Why do you hurt your brother?"

"I'm trying to help him!"

"By bashing his head in?"

"By releasing him from this…this *shit*!" Vinny tossed the skillet away and it clattered on the countertop. "It's all shit! The world is gone! Our band is gone! Half of my brother's head is gone! It's all gone. This is just….just leftovers."

"We're all leftovers, Vin," Evita said. "We're all that's left."

Vinny's head buzzed. He felt dizzy. He tried to sit but missed the chair and fell to the floor. Vance laughed again. Vinny put his arms over his head, drew his knees to his chest and screamed. He felt a tiny hand on his shoulder (*Pepper?*), but shrugged it off.

"How am I supposed to take care of him like *this*?" Vinny waved an arm at Vance. "He's…changed. He's all *fucked up*!"

"Fuck up!" Vance cheered.

"I told you, Vin…we've all changed, some more than others. We're *all* all fucked up," Evita said. "I'm stuck in a dead woman's body. Trish is blind. Vance has a major head injury. And Pepper…well, I don't really know Ms. Peppermint all that well, but she's clearly not the little girl she was before this started."

Pepper nodded at Evita and gave Vinny a sly smile.

"You're the only one who *hasn't* changed, Vin," Evita said. "We've all lost something except for you."

"I lost my brother…" Vinny mumbled. He glared at Trish. *She can't see you, fool!* "I lost him when Bobby Marks blew half his head away."

"Half-head!" Vance shouted. "Vinny!"

"Honestly, Vin, I was there when your brother had schizophrenic episodes and when he was an over-medicated mess and when he was suicidal," Evita said. "I don't know when you lost your brother, man, but he was gone *then*. Stop trying to control Vance and accept him for who he is *now*."

Vinny stared into Vance's wide, wet, idiotic smile. When did he lose his brother? Before The Dunwich Horrors? Before they'd lost Pegdick? Back in school? Vinny's parents and brother were so similar...until they became something else.

Something is always turning into something else, bro. Vance's voice chimed in Vinny's head—it would never go away. *Roll with the changes, like REO Speedwagon.*

But how could he love Vance now?

With your whole heart. Same as always. Dumb ass.

"Vinny! Mad!" Vance banged on the kitchen table.

"I'm sorry I lost my temper, Vance," Vinny said. "I'm sorry I hit you with a skillet."

"Eggs!" Vance shouted.

"I'm sorry, Vance," Vinny said. He looked around, apologizing to everyone in the room. "I'm sorry. I lost myself."

"This is the second, third...fourth time this has happened, Vin," Evita said. "We can't have a killer among us. We can't have an...unstable element."

The idea of being left behind never occurred to Vinny.

"Of course," he nodded. "It won't happen again."

"I'm not sure I believe you," Evita said. Her gaze stopped Vinny's heart. "We've all changed, Vin. But I'm not sure you're capable of it."

Vinny shook his head. "No, please...please..."

"Yesterday!" Vance shouted, though it sounded more

like *yesterbay*. "Music!"

Evita shook her head.

"You're right, Vance. There was music yesterday," she said. "And maybe there'll be music again tomorrow."

"No," Vinny said. "He wants to sing 'Yesterday' by The Beatles."

Trish smiled.

"That's a good one," she said.

"How does it go, Momma?" Pepper asked.

Trish sang the first verse, badly, and Vance shocked everyone—except Vinny—by singing the second verse loud and clear. Evita looked sad when Vance sang about being half the man he used to be, but joined in on the turnaround, tapping a shuffling beat on the kitchen table with her hands, and Vinny saw Thom emerge for the first time. Trish harmonized on the chorus, badly, and Vance sang the third verse. He never looked happier.

Pepper picked up her laundry bag and sat next to Vinny. She whispered in his ear.

"You need to help me tune this."

She opened the laundry bag and pulled out the strangest, most terrible stringed instrument Vinny ever saw, made of bleached bone, dried skin, and strings...dear God... A fun fact popped into Vinny's head (*"Early folk guitars were called 'gut strings,' because the strings were made of cat intestine!"*), followed by Vance's dry chuckle, *Ain't no cats down here but us, bro*!

Pepper cradled her instrument in her lap like a doll, a kitten, an infant. Perhaps Evita was right. There would be music again tomorrow. But Vinny shuddered to think what the tune might be.

Some songs demand sacrifice.

END

Rob Errera

ROB ERRERA IS A WRITER, editor, musician, and literary critic. His fiction, non-fiction, and essays have earned numerous awards. He lives in New Jersey with his wife, two kids, and a bunch of rescued dogs and cats. He blogs at **roberrera.com**, tweets **@haikubob,** and his work is available in both print and digital editions at all major online booksellers.

Non-Fiction
Autism Dad Vol. 1—Adventures In Raising An Autistic Son
Autism Dad Vol. 2—Tween Edition: Continuing Adventures in Autism, Adolescence, and Fatherhood.
Autism Dad Vol. 3—Life Skills & Life Lessons
Santa's Little Helper Wants To Eat Your Children
Fake News And Real Bullshit
Rock 'n' Roll And Comic Books Taught Me All I Know

Fiction
Tales of Franz Rock Terror
Hangman's Jam: A Symphony Of Terror
The Dunwich Horrors Die Tonight: Hangman's Jam, Vol II
Kiss The Sky Goodbye: Hangman's Jam, Vol III
Songs In the Key Of Madness: Variations On Hangman's Jam
Sensual Nightmares: Tales From The Palomino, Vol. I
The Mud Man: Mud Chronicles, Vol. 1
Other Fiction
Eight Strange Stories

More reading excitement from ...

  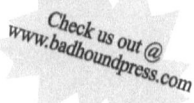

Hangman's Jam
by Rob Errera

Some songs stick in your head. Others consume your soul. A song called "Hangman's Jam" opens the doorway between dimensions, and bar band bassist Bobby Marks rides this strange tune to super stardom, but finds his newfound responsibilities as husband clash with a surreal world of addiction and overdoses, on stage deaths, internet sex scandals, studio ghosts and cosmic monsters. It's a symphony of terror.

Our Great Abbess
by C.L. Holmes

A secluded convent at the precipice of terror! Witness: Villainous nobles, vengeful spirits, intriguing priests, treacherous rogues, sadistic rape-fiends, love-smitten spies ... and still ever more violent menace and subtle dangers hounding the nuns of the St. Agnes convent to extinction ... in what descends into the most harrowing moment of the order's history, as the world's evils come to destroy them all. This is Great Abbess' dark, cruel origin.

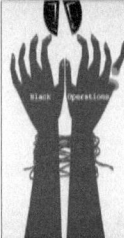

Black Operations
by Tommit Brahm

Why are there so many dead Tangerian politicians just before the election? The answer is not as simple as it seems. Shawn Harrison's mission to discover the cause has him crossing paths with a rogue agent, tracking down the most beautiful woman he has ever met, and throws him against a strange, ide-cold villain of incalculable evil ... and his pulse-pounding adventure is just one of many in this thrilling tale of espionage, romance and horror..

Sensual Nightmares
by Rob Errera

Eight linked tales of terror guaranteed to give you sensual nightmares! The worlds of H.P. Lovecraft, Margaret Atwood and Geoffrey Chaucer collide with fetish videos, peep booths and live sex shows in this erotic horror mash-up. Pull up a chair, order a shot and pepare yourself for hardcore horror!
Includes the full-length novella "The Porn Maid's Tale."